"You Had Better Get It Over With".

tegeus-Cromis raised the nameless sword for the fatal stroke. He spat down into the face before him: but it was still the face of a friend. He shuddered with conflicting desires.

He raised his eyes to the ring of Northmen who waited to take his blood in exchange for Trinor's. He moaned with rage and frustration, but he could not drown out the voices of the past within him. *"Keep* your bloody champion!" he cried. "Kill him yourself, for he'll betray you, too!" And he turned his horse on its haunches, smashed into their astonished ranks like a storm from the desert, and howled away into the honest carnage of the battlefield as if the gates of hell had opened behind him.

A long time later, at the foot of the knoll in the center of the valley, two Northern pikemen unhorsed him, and wondered briefly why he apologized as he rolled from his wrecked animal to kill them.

PUBLISHED BY POCKET BOOKS NEW YORK

The Pastel City

M. John Harrison

Volume I of The Tales of Viriconium

A TIMESCAPE BOOK

PUBLISHED BY POCKET BOOKS NEW YORK

A Timescape Book published by
POCKET BOOKS, a Simon & Schuster division of
GULF & WESTERN CORPORATION
1230 Avenue of the Americas, New York, N.Y. 10020

ISBN: 0-671-83584-X

First Timescape Books printing April, 1981

10 9 8 7 6 5 4 3 2 1

This is for:
MAURICE AND LYNETTE COLLIER,
LINDA AND JOHN LUTKIN.

The Pastel City

PROLOGUE

On the Empire of Viriconium

Some seventeen notable empires rose in the Middle Period of Earth. These were the Afternoon Cultures. All but one are unimportant to this narrative, and there is little need to speak of them save to say that none of them lasted for less than a millennium, none for more than ten; that each extracted such secrets and obtained such comforts as its nature (and the nature of the Universe) enabled it to find; and that each fell back from the Universe in confusion, dwindled, and died.

The last of them left its name written in the stars, but no-one who came later could read it. More important, perhaps, it built enduringly despite its failing strength—leaving certain technologies that, for good or ill, retained their properties of operation for well over a thousand years. And more important still, it *was* the last of the Afternoon Cultures, and was followed by Evening, and by Viriconium.

For five hundred years or more after the final collapse of the Middle Period, Viriconium (it had not that name, yet) was a primitive huddle of communities bounded by the sea in the West and South, by the unexplored lands in the East, and the Great Brown Waste of the North.

The wealth of its people lay entirely in salvage. They possessed no science, but scavenged the deserts of rust that had been originally the industrial complexes of the last of the Afternoon Cultures: and since the largest deposits of metal and machinery and ancient weapons lay in the Great Brown Waste, the Northern Tribes held them. Their loose empire had twin hubs, Glenluce and Drunmore, bleak sprawling townships where intricate and beautiful machines of unknown function were processed crudely into swords and tribal chieftains fought drunkenly over possession of the deadly *baans* unearthed from the desert.

They were fierce and jealous. Their rule of the Southerners was unkind, and, eventually, insupportable.

The destruction of this pre-Viriconium culture, and the wresting of power from the Northmen was accomplished by Borring-Na-Lecht, son of a herdsman of the Monar Mountains, who gathered the Southerners, stiffened their spines with his rural but powerful rhetoric, and in a single week gutted both Drunmore and Glenluce.

He was a hero. During his lifetime, he united the tribes, drove the Northmen into the mountains and tundra beyond Glenluce and built the city-fortress of

Duirinish on the edge of the Metal-salt Marsh where rusts and chemicals weather-washed from the Great Brown Waste collected in bogs and poisonous fens and drained into the sea. Thus, he closed the Low Leedale against the remnants of the Northern regime, protecting the growing Southern cities of Soubridge and Lendalfoot.

But his greatest feat was the renovation of Viriconium, hub of the last of the Afternoon Cultures, and he took it for his capital—building where necessary, opening the time-choked thoroughfares, adding artifacts and works of art from the rust deserts, until the city glowed almost as it had done half a millennium before. From it, the empire took its name. Borring was a hero.

No other hero came until Methven. During the centuries after Borring's death, Viriconium consolidated, grew plump and rich, concerned itself with wealth, internal trade and minor political hagglings. What had begun well, in fire and blood and triumph, lost its spirit.

For four hundred years the empire sat still while the Northmen licked their wounds and nourished their resentments. A slow war of attrition began, with the Southerners grown spineless again, the Northmen schooled to savagery by their harsh cold environment. Viriconium revered stability and poetry and wine-merchants: its wolf-cousins, only revenge. But, after a century of slow encroachment, the wolves met one who, if not of their kind, understood their ways . . .

Methven Nian came to the throne of Viriconium to find the supply of metals and Old Machines declining. He saw that a Dark Age approached; he wished to rule something more than a scavenger's empire. He drew to him young men who also saw this, and who respected the threat from the North. For him, they struck and struck again at the lands beyond Duirinish, and became known as the Northkillers, the Order of Methven, or, simply, *the Methven.*

There were many of them and many died. They fought with ruthlessness and a cold competence. They were chosen each for a special skill: thus, Norvin Trinor for his strategies, Tomb the Dwarf for his skill with mechanics and energy-weapons, Labart Tane for his knowledge of Northern folkways, Benedict Paucemanly for his aeronautics, tegeus-Cromis because he was the finest swordsman in the land.

For his span, Methven Nian halted the decay: he taught the Northmen to fear him; he instituted the beginnings of a science independent of the Old Technologies; he conserved what remained of that technology. He made one mistake, but that one was grievous.

In an attempt to cement a passing alliance with some of the Northern Tribes, he persuaded his brother Methvel, whom he loved, to marry their Queen, Balquhider. On the failure of the treaty two years later, this wolf-woman left Methvel in their chambers, drowning in his own blood, his eyes plucked out with a costume-pin, and, taking their daughter, Canna Moidart, fled. She schooled the child to see its future as the crown of a combined empire; to make pretense on Methven's death to the throne of Viriconium.

Nurtured on the grievances of the North, the Moidart aged before her time, and fanned in secret sparks of discontent in both North and South.

So it was that when Methven died—some said

partly of the lasting sorrow at Methvel's end—there were two Queens to pretend to the throne: Canna Moidart, and Methven's sole heir Methvet, known in her youth as Jane. And the knights of the Order of Methven, seeing a strong empire that had little need of their violent abilities, confused and saddened by the death of their King, scattered.

Canna Moidart waited a decade before the first twist of the knife . . .

1

tegeus-Cromis, sometime soldier and sophisticate of Viriconium, the Pastel City, who now dwelt quite alone in a tower by the sea and imagined himself a better poet than swordsman, stood at early morning on the sand-dunes that lay between his tall home and the gray line of the surf. Like swift and tattered scraps of rag, black gulls sped and fought over his downcast head. It was a catastrophe that had driven him from his tower, something that he had witnessed from its topmost room during the night.

He smelled burning on the offshore wind. In the distance, faintly, he could hear dull and heavy explosions: and it was not the powerful sea that shook the dunes beneath his feet.

Cromis was a tall man, thin and cadaverous. He had slept little lately, and his green eyes were tired in the dark sunken hollows above his high, prominent cheekbones.

He wore a dark green velvet cloak, spun about him like a cocoon against the wind; a tabard of antique leather set with iridium studs over a white kid shirt; tight mazarine velvet trousers and high, soft boots of pale blue suede. Beneath the heavy cloak, his slim and deceptively delicate hands were curled into fists, weighted, as was the custom of the time, with heavy rings of nonprecious metals intagliated with involved cyphers and sphenograms. The right fist rested on the pommel of his plain long sword, which, contrary to the fashion of the time, had no name. Cromis, whose lips were thin and bloodless, was more possessed by the essential qualities of things than by their names; concerned with the reality of Reality, rather than with the names men give it.

He worried more, for instance, about the beauty of the city that had fallen during the night than he did that it was Viriconium, the Pastel City. He loved it more for its avenues paved in pale blue and for its alleys that were not paved at all than he did for what its citizens chose to call it, which was often Viricon the Old and The Place Where The Roads Meet.

He had found no rest in music, which he loved, and now he found none on the pink sand.

For a while he walked the tideline, examining the objects cast up by the sea: paying particular attention to a smooth stone here, a translucent spiny shell there; picking up a bottle the color of his cloak, throwing down a branch whitened and peculiarly carved by the water. He watched the black gulls, but their cries depressed him. He listened to the cold wind in the rowan woods around his tower, and he shivered. Over the pounding of the high tide, he heard the dull concussions of falling Viriconium. And even when he stood in

15

the surf, feeling its sharp acid sting on his cheek, lost in its thunder, he imagined it was possible to hear the riots in the pastel streets, the warring factions, and voices crying for Young Queen, Old Queen.

He settled his russet shovel hat more firmly; crossed the dunes, his feet slipping in the treacherous sand; and found the white stone path through the rowans to his tower, which also had no name: though it was called by some after the stretch of seaboard on which it stood, that is, Balmacara. Cromis knew where his heart and his sword lay—but he had thought that all finished with and he had looked forward to a comfortable life by the sea.

When the first of the refugees arrived, he knew who had won the city, or the shell of it that remained: but the circumstances of his learning gave him no pleasure.

It was before noon, and he had still not decided what to do.

He sat in his highest room (a circular place, small, the walls of which were lined with leather and shelves of books: musical and scientific objects, astrolabes and lutes, stood on its draped stone tables; it was here that he worked at his songs), playing softly an instrument that he had got under strange circumstances some time ago, in the east. Its strings were taut and harsh, and stung his finger-ends; its tone was high and unpleasant and melancholy; but that was his mood. He played in a mode forgotten by all but himself and certain desert musicians, and his thoughts were not with the music.

From the curved window of the room he could see out over the rowans and the gnarled thorn to the road that ran from the unfortunate city to Duirinish in the north-east. Viriconium itself was a smoke-haze above the eastern horizon and an unpleasant vibration in the foundations of the tower. He saw a launch rise out of that haze, a speck like a trick of the eye.

It was well-known in the alleys of the city, and in remoter places, that, when tegeus-Cromis was nervous or debating within himself, his right hand strayed constantly to the pommel of his nameless sword: then was hardly the time to strike: and there was no other. He had never noticed it himself. He put down his instrument and went over to the window.

The launch gained height, gyring slowly: flew a short way north while Cromis strained his eyes, and then began to make directly toward Balmacara. For a little while, it appeared to be stationary, merely growing larger as it neared the tower.

When it came close enough to make out detail, Cromis saw that its faceted crystal hull had been blackened by fire, and that a great rift ran the full length of its starboard side. Its power plant (the secret of which, like many other things, had been lost a thousand years before the rise of Viriconium, so that Cromis and his contemporaries lived on the corpse of an ancient science, dependent on the enduring relics of a dead race) ran with a dreary insectile humming where it should have been silent. A pale halo of St. Elmo's Fire crackled from its bow to its stern, coruscating. Behind the shattered glass of its canopy, Cromis could see no pilot, and its flight was erratic: it yawed and pitched aimlessly, like a waterbird on a quiet current.

Cromis' knuckles stood out white against the sweat-darkened leather of his sword hilt as the vehicle dived, spun wildly, and lost a hundred feet in less than a second. It scraped the tops of the rowans, shuddered like a dying animal, gained a few precious, hopeless feet. It ploughed into the wood, discharging enormous sparks, its motors wailing. A smell of ozone was in the air.

Before the wreckage had hit the ground, Cromis was out of the high room, and, cloak streaming about him, was descending the spiral staircase at the spine of the tower.

At first, he thought the entire wood had caught fire.

Strange, motionless pillars of flame sprang up before him, red and gold, and burnished copper. He thought, "We are at the mercy of these old machines, we know so little of the forces that drive them." He threw up his arm to guard his face against the heat:

And realized that most of the flames he saw were merely autumn leaves, the wild colors of the dying year. Only two or three of the rowans were actually burning. They gave off a thick white smoke and a not-unpleasant smell. So many different kinds of fire, he thought. Then he ran on down the white stone path, berating himself for a fool.

Unknown to him, he had drawn his sword.

Having demolished a short lane through the rowans, the launch lay like an immense split fruit, the original rent in its side now a gaping black hole through which he could discern odd glimmers of light. It was as long as his tower was tall. It seemed unaffected by its own discharges, as if the webs of force that latticed the crystal shell were of a different order than that of heat; something cold, but altogether powerful. Energy drained from it, and the discharges became fewer. The lights inside its ruptured hull danced and changed position, like fireflies of an uncustomary color.

No man could have lived through that, Cromis thought. He choked on the rowan smoke.

He had begun to turn sadly away when a figure staggered out of the wreckage toward him, swaying.

The survivor was dressed in charred rags, his face blackened by beard and grime. His eyes shone startlingly white from shadowed pits, and his right arm was a bloody, bandaged stump. He gazed about him, regarding the burning rowans with fear and bemusement: he, too, seemed to see the whole wood as a furnace. He looked directly at Cromis.

"Help!" he cried, "Help!"

He shuddered, stumbled, and fell. A bough dropped from one of the blazing trees. Fire licked at the still body.

Cromis hurled himself forward, hacking a path through the burning foliage with his sword. Cinders settled on his cloak, and the air was hot. Reaching the motionless body, he sheathed the blade, hung the man over his shoulders like a yoke, and started away from the crippled launch. There was an unpleasant, exposed sensation crawling somewhere in the back of his skull. He had made a hundred yards, his breath coming hard as the unaccustomed exertion began to tell, when the vehicle exploded. A great soundless gout of white cold fire, locked in the core of the launch by a vanished art, dissipated itself as pure light, a millennium after its confinement.

It did him no harm: or none that he could recognize.

As he reached the gates of Balmacara, something detached itself from the raggy clothing of the survivor and fell to the ground: a drawstring pouch of goat shagreen, full of coin. Possibly, in some dream, he

19

heard the thud and ring of his portion of the fallen city. He shifted and moaned. There was at least one more bag of metal on him: it rattled dully as he moved. tegeus-Cromis curled his upper lip. He had wondered why the man was so heavy.

Once inside the tower, he recovered quickly. Cromis ministered to him in one of the lower rooms, giving him stimulants and changing the blood-stiffened bandage on the severed arm, which had been cauterized negligently and was beginning to weep a clear, unhealthy fluid. The room, which was hung with weapons and curiosities of old campaigns, began to smell of burned cloth and pungent drugs.

The survivor woke, flinched when he saw Cromis, his remaining hand clawing at the blue embroidered silks of the wall-bed on which he lay. He was a heavy-boned man of medium height, and seemed to be of the lower merchant classes, a vendor of wine, perhaps, or women. The pupils of his black eyes were dilated, their whites large and veined with red. He seemed to relax a little. Cromis took his shoulders, and, as gently as he was able, pressed him down.

"Rest yourself," he told him. "You are in the tower of tegeus-Cromis, that some men call Balmacara. I must know your name if we are to talk."

The black eyes flickered warily round the walls. They touched briefly on a powered battle-axe that Cromis had got from his friend Tomb the Dwarf after the sea-fight at Mingulay in the Rivermouth campaign; moved to the gaudy green-and-gold standard of Thorisman Carlemaker, whom Cromis had defeated single-handed—and with regret, since he had no quarrel with the fine rogue—in the Mountains of Monadhliath; came finally to rest on the hilt of the intangible-bladed *baan* that had accidentally killed Cromıs' sister Galen. He looked from that to Cromis.

"I am Ronoan Mor, a merchant." There was open suspicion in his eyes and in his voice. He fumbled beneath his clothing. "You have strange tastes," he said, nodding at the relics on the wall. Cromis, noting the fumbling hand, smiled.

"Your coin fell as I carried you from your launch, Ronoan Mor." He pointed to where the three purses lay on an inlaid table. "You will find that all of it is present. How are things in the Pastel City?"

It could not have been the money that worried Ronoan Mor, for the wariness did not leave his face. And that was a surprising thing. He bared his teeth.

"Hard," he muttered, gazing bitterly at his severed limb. He hawked deep in his throat, and might have spat had there been a receptacle. "The young bitch holds steady, and we were routed. But—"

There was such a look of fanaticism in his eyes that Cromis' hand, of its own accord, began to caress the pommel of the nameless sword. He was more puzzled than angered by Mor's insult to the Young Queen. If a man normally given to dreaming of bargain prices and a comfortable retirement (if of anything at all) could show this measure of devotion to a political cause, then things were truly out of joint in the land. Immediately, he found himself thinking: And did you need to know that, Sir Cromis? Is it not enough that the Pastel Towers shudder and fall overnight? There must be further proof?

But he smiled and interrupted Mor, saying softly, "That is not so hard, sir."

For a moment, the survivor went on as if he had

not heard: "—But she cannot hold for long when Canna Moidart's northern allies join with those patriots left in the city—"

There was a feverish, canting tone in his voice, as though he repeated a creed. Sweat broke out on his brow, and spittle appeared on his lips. "Aye, we'll have her then, for sure! And caught between two blades—"

He held his tongue and studied Cromis closely, squinting. Cromis stared levelly back, endeavoring not to show how this intelligence affected him. Mor clawed himself into a sitting position, trembling with the effort.

"Wise to reveal yourself, tegeus-Cromis!" he cried suddenly, like an orator who singles one man from a crowd of rustics. "Where does *your* service lie?"

"You tire yourself needlessly," murmured Cromis. "It matters little to me," he lied, "for, as you see, I am a recluse. But I admit myself interested in this tale of the Old Queen and her northern cousins. She has a large following, you say?"

As if in answer, Ronoan Mor's good hand fumbled in his clothing again. And this time, it drew forth a twelve-inch sliver of flickering green light that hissed and crackled:

A *baan*.

He drew back his lips, held the ancient weapon stiffly before him (all men fear them, even their users), and snarled, "Large enough for you, sir. You see—" He glanced sideways at the trophies on the wall "—others may hold forceblades. *Northerners,* they tell me, have many such. With whom does your service lie, tegeus-Cromis?" He twitched the *baan* so it sparked and spat. *"Tell* me! Your evasions weary me—"

Cromis felt perspiration trickling under his armpits. He was no coward, but he had been long away from violence: and though the *baan* was in poor condition, the energies that formed its blade running low, it would still slice steel, make play of bone and butter of flesh.

"I would remind you, Ronoan Mor," he said quietly, "that you are ill. Your arm. Fever makes you hasty. I have given you succour——"

"This to your succour!" shouted Mor, and spat. "Tell me, or I'll open you from crutch to collar-bone."

The *baan* flickered like an electric snake.

"You are a fool, Ronoan Mor. Only a fool insults a man's queen under that man's hospitable roof."

Mor flung his head back and howled like a beast.

He lunged blindly.

Cromis whirled, tangled his cloak about hand and *baan*. As the blade cut free, he crouched, rolled, changed direction, rolled again, so that his body became a blur of motion on the stone-flagged floor. The nameless sword slid from its sheath: and he was tegeus-Cromis the Northkiller once again, Companion of the Order of Methven and Bane of Carlemaker.

Confused, Mor backed up against the head of the bed, his slitted eyes fixed on the crouching swordsman. He was breathing heavily.

"Forget it, man!" said Cromis. "I will accept your apologies. Your illness wears you. I have no use for this foolishness. The Methven do not slaughter merchants."

Mor threw the forceblade at him.

tegeus-Cromis, who had thought never to fight again, *laughed*.

As the *baan* buried itself in the trophy wall, he sprang forward, so that his whole long body followed the line of the nameless sword.

A choked cry, and Ronoan Mor was dead.

tegeus-Cromis, who fancied himself a better poet

than armsman, stood over the corpse, watched sadly the blood well on to the blue silk bed, and cursed himself for lack of mercy.

"I stand for Queen Jane, merchant," he said. "As I stood for her father. It is that simple."

He wiped the blade of the sword with no name and went to prepare himself for a journey to the Pastel City, no longer plagued by dreams of a quiet life.

Before he left, another thing happened, a welcome thing.

He did not expect to see his tower again. In his skull, there was a premonition: Canna Moidart and her true kinsmen burned down from the voracious north with wild eyes and the old weapons, come to extract vengeance from the city and empire that had ousted them a century since. The savage blood ran true: though Canna Moidart was of Methven's line, being the daughter of his brother Methvel, old quarrels ran in her veins from her mother Balquhider's side; and she had expected the sovereignty on the death of her uncle. Viriconium had grown fat and mercantile while Methven grew old and Moidart fermented discontent in kingdom and city. And the wolves of the north had sharpened their teeth on their grievances.

He did not expect to see Balmacara again: so he stood in his topmost room and chose an instrument to take with him. Though the land go down into death and misrule, and tegeus-Cromis of the nameless sword with it, there should be some poetry before the end.

The fire in the rowan wood had died. Of the crystal launch, nothing remained but a charred glade an acre across. The road wound away to Viriconium.

Some measure of order had prevailed there, for the smoke haze had left the horizon and the foundations of the tower no longer trembled. He hoped fervently that Queen Jane still prevailed, and that the calm was not that of a spent city, close to death.

Along the road, gray dust billowing about them, rode some thirty or forty horsemen, heading for Balmacara.

He could not see their standard, but he put down the gourd-shaped instrument from the east and went to welcome them; whether with words or with his blade, he did not much care.

He was early at the gates. Empty yet, the road ran into the rowans, to curve sharply and disappear from sight. A black bird skittered through the leaves, sounding its alarm call; sat on a branch and regarded him suspiciously from beady, old man's eyes. The sound of hooves drew nearer.

Mounted on a pink roan mare fully nineteen hands high and caparisoned in bright yellow, the first horseman came into view.

He was a massive man, heavy in the shoulders and heavier in the hips, with thin, long blond hair that curled anarchically about a jowled and bearded face. He wore orange breeches tucked into oxblood boots, and a violet shirt, the sleeves of which were slashed and scolloped.

On his head was a floppy-brimmed rustic hat of dark brown felt, which the wind constantly threatened to take from him.

He was roaring out a Duirinish ballad which enumerated the hours of the clock as chimed inside a brothel.

Cromis' shout of greeting drove the black bird entirely away.

25

He ran forward, sheathing his sword and crying, "Grif! *Grif!*"

He gathered up the reins beneath the roan mare's bit, hauled her to a halt and pounded one of the ox-blood boots with the heel of his hand.

"Grif, I had not thought to see you again! I had not thought any of us were left!"

2

"No, Cromis, there are a few left. Had you not gone to earth after your sister Galen's accident, and then crept secretly back to this empty place, you would have seen that Methven made due provision for the Order: he did not intend it to die with his own death. A few left: but truthfully a few, and those scattered."

They sat in the high room, Birkin Grif sprawled with a mug of distilled wine, his boots on a priceless onyx table, while Cromis plucked half-heartedly at the eastern gourd or paced restlessly the floor. The chink of metal on metal filtered from the courtyard far beneath, where Grif's men prepared a meal, watered their horses. It was late afternoon, the wind had dropped, and the rowans were still.

"Do you know then of Norvin Trinor, or of Tomb the Dwarf?" asked Cromis.

"Ho! Who knows of Tomb even when the times are

uncomplicated? He searches for old machines in deserts of rust, no doubt. He lives, I am sure, and will appear like a bad omen in due course. As for Trinor, I had hoped you would know: Viriconium was always his city, and you live quite close."

Cromis avoided the big man's eyes.

"Since the deaths of Galen and Methven, I have seen no-one. I have been . . . I have been solitary, and hoped to remain so. Have some more wine."

He filled Grif's cup.

"You are a brooder," said Grif, "and some day you will hatch eggs." He laughed. He choked on his drink. "What is your appraisal of the situation?"

Away from thoughts of Galen, Cromis felt on firmer ground.

"You know that there were riots in the city, and that the queen held her ground against Canna Moidart's insurgents?"

"Aye. I expect to break the heads of malcontents. We were on our way to do that when we noticed the smoke about your tower. You'll join us, of course?"

Cromis shook his head.

"A cordial invitation to a skull-splitting, but there are other considerations," he said. "I received intelligence this morning that the Moidart rides from the north. Having sown her seeds, she comes harvesting. She brings an army of northmen, headed by her mother's kin, and you know that brood have angered themselves since Borring dispossessed them and took the land for Viricon. Presumably, she gathers support on the way."

Birkin Grif heaved himself from his chair. He stamped over to the window and looked down at his men, his breath wheezing. He turned to Cromis, and his heavy face was dark.

"Then we had better to ride, and swiftly. This is a bad thing. How far has the Moidart progressed? Has the Young Queen marshalled her forces?"

Cromis shrugged.

"You forget, my friend. I have been a recluse, preferring poetry to courts and swords. My . . . informant . . . told me nothing but what I have told you. He died a little later. He was in some part responsible for the smoke you saw." He poured himself a mug of wine, and went on:

"What I counsel is this: that you should take your company and go north, taking the fastest route and travelling lightly. Should the queen have prepared an army, you will doubtless overhaul it before any significant confrontation. Unless a Methven be already in charge of it, you must offer (offer only: people forget, and we have not the king to back us any more) your generalship.

"If there is no army, or if a Methven commands, then lead your men as a raiding force: locate the Moidart and harry her flanks."

Grif laughed. "Aye, prick her. I have the skill for that, all right. And my men, too." He became serious. "But it will take time, weeks possibly, for me to reach her. Unless she already knocks at the door."

"I think not. That must be your course, however long. Travelling by the canny routes, news of her coming would be a full three weeks ahead of her. An army cannot take the hill ways. With speed, we can hope to engage her well before she reaches Viriconium."

"What of yourself, in these weeks we scatter like minutes?"

"Today, I leave for the city. There I will arrange the backing of Queen Jane for the Methven and also seek Trinor, for he would be an asset. If an army has been sent (and I cannot think the queen as ill-formed as I: there must be one), I will join you, probably at Duirinish, bringing any help I can."

"Fair enough, Cromis. You will need a couple of men in the unquiet city. I'll detail—"

Cromis held up his hand.

"I'll ride alone, Grif. Am I hard pressed, it will be useful practice. I have grown out of the way of fighting."

"Always the brooder." Grif returned to the window and bawled down into the courtyard, "Go to sleep, you skulkers! Three hours, and we ride north!"

Grif had not changed. However he lived, he lived it full. Cromis stood by him at the window and clapped his meaty shoulder.

"Tell me, Grif: what has been your business all these years?"

Grif bellowed with laughter, which seemed to infect his men. They milled about the courtyard, laughing too, although they could not have heard the question.

"Something as befits a Methven in peacetime, brooder. Or as you may have it, nothing as befits a Methven at any time. I have been smuggling distilled wine of low and horrible quality to peasants in the Cladich marshes, whose religion forbids them drink it . . ."

Cromis watched Grif's ragged crew disappear into the darkness at a stiff pace, their cloaks flapping out behind them. He waved once to the colorful figure of Grif himself, then turned to his horse, which was breathing mist into the cold night. He checked the girth and saddlebags, settled the eastern instrument across his back. He shortened his stirrups for swift riding.

With the coming of darkness, the winds had returned to Balmacara: the rowans shook continuously,
hissing and rustling; Cromis' shoulder-length black
hair was blown about his face. He looked back at the
tower, bulking dark against the cobalt sky. The surf
growled behind it. Out of some strange sentiment, he
had left the light burning in the upper room.

But the *baan* that had killed his sister, he had in
an insulated sheath next to his skin, because he knew
he would not come again, riding to the light out of
battle, to Balmacara in the morning.

Refugees packed the Viriconium road like a torchlit
procession in some lower gallery of Hell. Cromis
steered his nervous beast at speed past caravans of
old men pushing carts laden with clanking domestic
implements and files of women carrying or leading
young children. House animals scuttled between the
wheels of the carts.

The faces he passed were blank and frightened,
overlit and gleaming in the flaring unsteady light of
the torches. Some of them turned from him, surrepti-
tiously making religious signs (a brief writhe of the
fingers for Borring, whom some regarded as a god, a
complicated motion of the head for the Colpy). He
was at a loss to account for this. He thought that they
were the timid and uncommitted of the city, driven
away by fear of the clashing factions, holding no brief
for either side.

He entered the city by its twelfth gate, the Gate of
Nigg, and there was no gatekeeper to issue even the
customary token challenge.

His habitually morose mood shifted to the sombre
as he took the great radial road Proton Circuit, paved

with an ancient resilient material that absorbed the sound of his horse's hooves.

About him rose the Pastel Towers, tall and gracefully shaped to mathematical curves, tinted pale blue or fuchsia or dove-gray. They reached up for hundreds of feet, cut with quaint and complex designs that some said were the highpoint of an inimitable art, thought by others to be representations of the actual geometrics of Time.

Several of them were scarred and blackened by fire. Some were gutted and broken.

Seeing so much beauty brought down in this way, he was convinced that a change had come about in the essential nature of things, and that they could never be the same again.

Proton Circuit became a spiral that wound a hundred yards into the air, supported by slim and delicate pillars of black stone. At the summit of the spiral lay the palace of the Young Queen, that had been Methven's hall. A smaller building than most in that city, it was shaped like a filigree shell, built entirely of a pure white metal that vibrated and sang. Before its high bright arch stood guards in charcoal livery, who made stringent demands on him to reveal his identity and business.

They found it difficult to believe him a Methven (memories had indeed grown dim, for their chief objection to his claim was that he came with no ceremony or circumstance) and for some time refused him entrance: a circumspection he could only applaud.

He remembered certain passwords known only to the guards of the city.

He made his way along corridors of pale, fluctuating light, passing strange, precious objects that might have been animated sculptures or machines, excavated from ruined cities in the Rust Desert beyond Duirinish.

Queen Jane awaited him in a tall room floored with cinnabar-veined crystal and having five false windows that showed landscapes to be found nowhere in the kingdom.

Shambling slowly among the curtains of light and finely-wrought furniture was one of the giant albino megatheria of the southern forests: great sloth-like beasts, fifteen feet high when they stood upright (which was rarely) and armed with terrible cutting claws, though they were vegetarian and amiable. The Queen's beast wore an iridium collar, and its claws were sheathed in clear thick resin. Seeing Cromis, it ambled up to him in a sleepy manner, and gazed myopically at him. Patterns of light moved across its shining pelt.

"Leave him, Usheen," said a small, musical voice.

Cromis turned his eyes from the megatherium to the dais at the south end of the room.

Queen Jane of Viriconium, Methvet Nian, whom he had last seen as a child at Methven's court, was seventeen years of age. She sat on a simple throne and regarded him steadily with violet eyes. She was tall and supple, clad in a gown of russet velvet, and her skin was neither painted nor jeweled. The ten identical rings of Neap glittered from her long fingers. Her hair, which recalled the color of the autumn rowans of Balmacara, hung in soft waves to her waist, coiled about her breasts.

"Queen Jane," said Cromis and bowed.

She buried her fingers in the thick fur of the megatherium, and whispered to it. The false windows flickered with strange scenes. She looked up.

"Is it really you, Lord Cromis?" she said, strange expression crossing her pale triangular features.

"Have I changed so much, madam?"

"Not much, Lord Cromis: you were a stiff and sombre man, even when you sang, and you are that still. But I was very young when we last met—"

Suddenly, she laughed, rose from the throne and came gracefully down to take his hands. Cromis saw that her eyes were moist.

"—And I think I preferred Tomb the Dwarf in those days," she went on, "for he brought me the most wonderful things from his favorite ruins. Or Grif, perhaps, who told questionable tales and laughed a good deal—"

She drew him through the shifting light-sculptures to the dais, and made him sit down. The megatherium came to gaze wisely at him from brown, tranquil eyes. Methvet Nian sat on her simple throne, and the laughter left her.

"Oh, Cromis, why have none of you come before? These ten years, I have had need of your support. How many live?—I have seen none of you since my father's death."

"Grif lives, madam, for sure. Hours ago, he rode north at my request. He believes that Tomb and Trinor live also. Of the others I have heard nothing. We have come late to this, but you must not think too ill of us. I have come to discover just how late we are. What have been your moves to date?"

She shook her head musingly, so that her bright hair caught the light and moved like a fire.

"Two only, Cromis: I have held the city, though it has suffered; and I have dispatched Lord Waterbeck —who, though well-schooled, has not the strategies of one such as Norvin Trinor—with four regiments. We hope to engage my cousin before she reaches the Rust Desert."

"How long has Waterbeck been gone?"

"A week only. The launch fliers tell me he must reach her within another week and a half, for she travels surprisingly fast. Few of them have returned of late: they report launches destroyed in flight by energy-weapons, and their numbers are depleted.

"Our lines of communication grow thin, Cromis. It will be a dark age, should our last machines go down."

Again, she took his hand, silently drawing strength from him, and he knew that her young frame was frail for such weight of responsibility. He blamed himself, because that was his way.

"Cromis, can you do anything?"

"I start immediately," he said, trying to smile and finding the requisite muscles stiff from disuse. He gently disengaged her hands, for their cool touch had disturbed him.

"First I must locate Trinor, who may be somewhere in the city; although if that is so, I cannot say why he has not come to you before now. Then it will take me only a short time to come up with Grif, since I can take paths impassable to more than one rider.

"What I must have from you, my lady, is an authorization. Trinor or Grif must command that army when it meets the Moidart, or failing one of them, myself—this Waterbeck is a peacetime general, I would guess, and has not the experience of a Methven.

"You must not fear too greatly. Can it be done, we will do it, and fall bringing a victory about. Keep order here and faith with what Methven remain, even though we have not used you well."

She smiled, and the smile passed barriers he had not thought existed in his morose soul. She took off one of the steel rings of Neap and slid it on to his left index finger, which was hardly of greater diameter than her own, saying:

"This will be your authorization. It is traditional. Will you take a launch? They are swifter—"

He rose to leave, and found himself reluctant.

"No launch, my lady. Those, you must keep jealously, in case we fail. And I prefer to ride."

At the door of the room with five windows, he looked back through the drifting shapes and curtains of light, and it seemed to him that he saw a lost, beautiful child. She brought to mind his dead sister Galen, and he was not surprised: what shook him was that those memories somehow lacked the force they had had that morning. Cromis was a man who, like most recluses, thought he understood himself, and did not.

The great white sloth watched him out with almost human eyes, rearing up to its full height, its ambered claws glinting.

He stayed in the city for that night and another day. It was quiet, the streets empty and stunned. He had snippets of rumor that the Moidart's remaining supporters skulked the narrower alleys after dark and skirmished with groups of the city guard. He did not discount them, and kept a hand on the nameless sword. He expected to find Trinor somewhere in the old Artist's Quarter.

He inquired at several taverns there, but had no information. He grew progressively more impatient, and would have given up had not a derelict poet he met in the Bistro Californium advised him to take his queries to an address on Bread Street in the poorer part of the Quarter. It was said that blind Kristodulous had once rented a garret studio there.

He came to Bread Street at twilight. It was far removed from the palace and the Pastel Towers, a mean alley of aging, ugly houses, down which the wind funneled bitterly. Over the crazed rooftops, the sky bled. He shivered and thought of the Moidart, and the note of the wind became more urgent. He drew his cloak about him and rapped with the hilt of his sword on a weathered door.

He did not recognize the woman who opened it: perhaps the light was at fault.

She was tall, statuesque and graceful; her narrow face had an air of calm and the self-knowledge that may or may not come with suffering: but her blue robe was faded, patched here and there with material of quite another color, and her eyes were ringed with tired, lined flesh. He bowed out of courtesy.

"I seek Norvin Trinor," he said, "or news of him."

She peered into his face as if her eyes were weak, and said nothing. She stepped aside and motioned him to enter. He thought that a quiet, sad smile played about her firm mouth.

Inside, the house was dusty and dim, the furniture of rough, scrubbed deal. She offered him cheap, artificially-colored wine. They sat on opposite sides of a table and a silence. He looked from her discolored fingernails to the cobwebs in the windows, and said:

"I do not know you, madam. If you would be—"

Her weary eyes met his and still he did not know her. She got slowly to her feet and lit a squat hanging lamp.

"I am sorry, tegeus-Cromis. I should not have embarrassed you in this fashion. Norvin is not here. I—"

In the lamplight stood Carron Ban, the wife of Norvin Trinor, whom he had married after the fight against Carlemaker's brigands, twelve years before.

Time had gone against her, and she had aged beyond her years.

Cromis upset his chair as he got to his feet, sent it clattering across the floor. It was not the change in her that horrified him, but the poverty that had caused it.

"Carron! Carron! I did not know. What has happened here?"

She smiled, bitter as the wind.

"Norvin Trinor has been gone for nearly a year," she said. "You must not worry on my behalf. Sit down and drink the wine."

She moved away, avoiding his gaze, and stood looking into the darkness of Bread Street. Under the faded robe, her shoulders shook. Cromis came to her and put his hand on her arm.

"You should tell me," he said gently. "Come and tell me."

But she shrugged off the hand.

"Nothing to tell, my lord. He left no word. He seemed to have grown weary of the city, of me—"

"But Trinor would not merely have abandoned you! It is cruel of you to suggest such—"

She turned to face him and there was anger in her eyes.

"It was cruel of him to do it, Lord Cromis. I have heard nothing from him for a year. And now—now I *wish* to hear nothing of him. That is all finished, like many things that have not outlasted King Methven."

She walked to the door.

"If you would leave me, I would be pleased. Understand that I have nothing against you, Cromis; I should not have done this to you; but you bring memories I would rather not acknowledge."

"Lady, I—"

"Please go."

There was a terrible patience in her voice, in the set of her shoulders. She was brought down, and saw only that she would remain so. Cromis could not deny her. Her condition was painful to them both. That a Methven should cause such misery was hard to credit —that it should be Norvin Trinor was unbelievable. He halted at the door.

"If there is help you require—I have money—And the queen—"

She shook her head brusquely.

"I shall travel to my family in the south. I want nothing from this city or its empire." Her eyes softened. "I am sorry, tegeus-Cromis. You have meant nothing but good. I suggest you look for him in the north. That is the way he went.

"But I would have you remember this: he is not the friend you know. Something changed him after the death of Methven. He is not the man you knew."

"Should I find him—"

"I would have you carry no message. Goodbye."

She closed the door, and he was alone on that mean street with the wind. The night had closed in.

3

That night, haunted by three women and a grim future, Cromis of the nameless sword, who thought himself a better poet than fighter, left the Pastel City by
one of its Northern gates, his horse's hooves quiet on
the ancient paving. No-one hindered him.

Though he went prepared, he wore no armor save
a mail shirt, lacquered black as his short cloak and
leather breeches. It was the way of many of the Methven, who had found armor an encumbrance and not
protection against energy-blades. He had no helmet,
and his black hair streamed in the wind. The *baan*
was at his belt and his curious eastern instrument
across his back.

In a day, he came to the bleak hills of Monar that
lay between Viriconium and Duirinish, where the wind
lamented considerably some gigantic sorrow it was unable to put into words. He trembled the high paths

that wound over slopes of shale and between cold still lochans in empty corries. No birds lived there. Once he saw a crystal launch drift overhead, a dark smoke seeping from its hull. He thought a good deal of the strange actions of Norvin Trinor, but achieved no conclusions.

He went in this fashion for three days, and one thing happened to him while he traversed the summit of the Cruachan Ridge.

He had reached the third cairn on the ridge when a mist descended. Aware of the insecurity of the path in various places ahead, and noting that his beast was already prone to stumble on the loose, lichen-stained rock, he halted. The wind had dropped, and the silence made a peculiar ringing noise in his ears. It was comfortless and alien up there, impassable when the snow came, as were the lower valleys. He understood the Moidart's haste.

He found the cairn to be the tumbled ruins of an old four-faced tower constructed of a gray rock quite different from that beneath his feet. Three walls remained, and part of a ceiling. It had no windows. He could not guess its intended purpose, or why it was not built of native stone. It stood enigmatically among its own rubble, an eroded stub, and he wondered at the effort needed to transport its stones to such a height.

Inside, there were signs that other travelers of the Cruachan had been overtaken by the mist: several long-dead fires: the bare bones of small animals.

He tethered his horse, which had begun to shiver; fed it; and threw a light blanket over its hindquarters against the chill. He kindled a small fire and prepared a meal, then sat down to wait out the mist, taking up the eastern gourd and composing to its eery metallic tones a chanted lament. The mist coiled around him, sent cold, probing fingers into his meagre shelter. His words fell into the silence like stones into the absolute abyss:

"Strong visions: I have strong visions of this place in the empty times . . . Far below there are wavering pines . . . left the rowan elphin woods to fulminate on ancient headlands, dipping slowly into the glasen seas of evening . . . On the devastated peaks of hills we ease the barrenness into our thin bones like a foot into a tight shoe . . . The narrative of this place: other than the smashed arris of the ridge there are only sad winds and silences. . . . I lay on the cairn one more rock. . . . I am possessed by Time . . ."

He put the instrument away from him, disturbed by the echoes of his own voice. His horse shifted its feet uneasily. The mist wove subtle shapes, caught by a sudden faint breath of wind.

"tegeus-Cromis, tegeus-Cromis," said a reedy voice close at hand.

He leapt to his feet, the *baan* spitting and flickering in his left hand, the nameless sword greasing out of its dull sheath, his stance canny and murderous.

"There is a message for you."

He could see nothing. There was nothing but the mist. The horse skittered and plunged, snorting. The forceblade fizzed in the damp atmosphere.

"Come out!" he shouted, and the Cruachan echoed *out! out! out!*

"There is a message," repeated the voice.

He put his back against a worn wall and moved his head in a careful semi-circle, on the hunt. His breath came harsh. The fire blazed up red in the gray, unquiet vapors.

Perched on the rubble before him, its wicked head and bent neck underlit by the flames, was a bearded vulture—one of the huge, predatory lammergeyers of the lower slopes. In that gloom, it resembled a hunchbacked and spiteful old man. It spread and cupped a broad wing, fanning the fire, to preen its underfeathers. There was a strange sheen to its plumage; it caught the light in a way feathers do not.

It turned a small crimson eye on him. "The message is as follows," it said. Unlimbering both wings, it flapped noisily across the ruined room in its own wind, to perch on the wall by his head. His horse sidestepped nervously, tried to pull free from its tether, eyes white and rolling at the dark, powerful wings.

Cromis stood back warily, raised his sword. The lammergeyers were strong, and said by the herders to Monar to prefer children to lambs.

"If you will allow me:

"*tegeus-Cromis of Viriconium, which I take to be yourself, since you tally broadly with the description given, should go at once to the tower of Cellur.*" Here, it flexed its cruel claws on the cold gray stone, cocked its head, ruffled its feathers. "*Which he will find on the Girvan Bay in the South, a little East of Lendalfoot. Further—*"

Cromis felt unreal: the mist curled, the lammergeyer spoke, and he was fascinated. On Cruachan Ridge he might have been out of Time, lost: but was much concerned with the essential nature of things, and he kept his sword raised. He would have queried the bird, but it went on:

"*—Further, he is advised to let nothing hinder that journey, however pressing it may seem: for things*

*hang in a fine balance, and more is at stake than the
fate of a minor empire.*

"*This comes from Cellur of Girvan.* That is the message."

Who Cellur of Girvan might be, or what intelligence
he might have that overshadowed the fall of Viriconium
(or, indeed, how he had taught a vulture to
recognize a man he never could have met), Cromis
did not know. He waited his time, and touched the
neck of his horse to calm it.

"Should you feel you must follow another course, I
am instructed to emphasize the urgency of the matter,
and to stay with you until such time as you decide to
make the journey to Lendalfoot and Girvan. At intervals,
I shall repeat the message, in case it should become
obscured by circumstance.

"Meanwhile, there may be questions you wish to
ask. I have been provided with an excellent vocabulary."

With a taloned foot, it scratched the feathers behind
its head, and seemed to pay no more attention to
him. He sheathed his sword, seeing no threat. His beast
had quietened, so he walked back to the fire. The lammergeyer
followed. He looked into its glittering eyes.

"What are you?" he asked.

"I am a Messenger of Cellur."

"Who is he?"

"I have not been instructed in the description of
him."

"What is his purpose?"

"I have not been instructed in the description of
that."

"What is the exact nature of the threat perceived by
him?"

"He fears the *geteit chemosit.*"

The mist did not lift that day or that night. Though Cromis spent much of this time questioning the bird, he learned little; its answers were evasive and he could get nothing more from it than that unpleasant name.

The morning came gray and overcast, windy and sodden and damp. The sister-ridges of the Cruachan stretched away East and West like the ribs of a gigantic animal. They left the third cairn together, the bird wheeling and gyring high above him on the termagant air currents of the mountains, or coming to perch on the arch of his saddle. He was forced to warn it against the latter, for it upset the horse.

When the sun broke through, he saw that it was a bird of metal: every feather, from the long, tapering pinions of the great wide wings to the down on its hunched shoulders, had been stamped or beaten from wafer-thin iridium. It gleamed, and a very faint humming came from it. He grew used to it, and found that it could talk on many diverse subjects.

On his fifth day out of the Pastel City, he came in sight of Duirinish and the Rust Desert.

He came down the steep Lagach Fell to the source of the River Minfolin in High Leedale, a loamy valley two thousand feet up in the hills. He drank from the small, stone-ringed spring, listening to the whisper of the wind in the tall reed-grasses, then sought the crooked track from the valley down the slopes of Mam Sodhail to the city. The Minfolin chattered beside him as he went, growing stronger as it rushed over falls and rapids.

Low Leedale spread before him as he descended the last few hundred feet of Sodhail: a sweep of purple and brown and green quartered by gray stone walls and dotted with herders' crofts in which yellow lights were beginning to show. Through it ran the matured Minfolin, dark and slow; like a river of lead it flowed past the city at the north end of the valley, to lose and diffuse itself among the Metal-salt Marshes on the verge of the Rust Desert: from there, it drained westward into the sea.

Somber Duirinish, set between the stark hills and the great brown waste, had something of the nature of both: a bleakness.

A walled city of flint and black granite, built twenty generations before against the threat of the northern clans, it stood in a meander of the river, its cobbled roads inclining steeply among squat buildings to the central fastness, the castle within the city, Alves. Those walls that faced the Rust Desert rose vertically for two hundred feet, then sloped outwards. No welcome in Duirinish for northern men. As Cromis reached the Low Leedale, the great Evening Bell was tolling the seventh change of guard on the north wall. A pale mist clung to the surface of the river fingering the walls as it flowed past.

Camped about a mile south of the city, by the stone bridge over the Minfolin, were Birkin Grif's smugglers.

Their fires flared in the twilight, winking as the men moved between them. There was laughter, and the unmusical clank of cooking utensils. They had set a watch at the center of the bridge. Before attempting to cross, Cromis called the lammergeyer to him. Flapping out of the evening, it was a black cruciform silhouette on gray.

"Perch here," he told it, extending his forearm in the manner of a falconer, "and make no sudden movement."

His horse clattered over the bridge, steel striking sparks from flint. The bird was heavy on his arm, and its metal plumage glinted in the eastern afterglow. The guard gazed at it with wide eyes, but brought him without question to Grif, who was lounging in the firelight, chuckling to himself over some internal joke and eating raw calf's liver, a delicacy of his.

"That sort of bird makes poor eating," he said. "There must be more to this than meets the eye."

Cromis dismounted and gave his horse into the care of the guard. His limbs were stiff from the fell-journey, and the cooking smells of the encampment had made him aware of his hunger.

"Much more," he said. He hefted the lammergeyer, as if to fly it from his arm. "Repeat your message," he commanded it. Birkin Grif raised his eyebrows.

"tegeus-Cromis of Viriconium," began the bird reedily, *"should go at once to the tower of Cellur, which he will find—"*

"Enough," said Cromis. "Well, Grif?"

"A flock of these things has shadowed us for two days, flying high and circling. We brought one down, and it seemed to be made of metal, so we threw it in a river. A strange thing, that you might be good enough to tell me about while you eat."

Cromis nodded. "They are unlikely to trouble you again," he said. "Their purpose, apparently, has been fulfilled."

He allowed the lammergeyer to flap from his arm, and, massaging the place where its talons had clung to him, sat down next to Grif. He accepted a cup of distilled wine, and let it heat his throat. The camp had become quieter, and he could hear the mournful soughing of the wind about the ridges and peaks of Monar. The Minfolin murmured around the piers of the bridge. He began to feel comfortable as the warmth of fire and wine seeped through him.

"However," he said, "I should advise your men to shoot no more of them, should any appear. This Cellur may have odd means of redress."

From a place beside the fire, the lammergeyer cocked its head, presenting to them a blank red eye.

"You did not find Trinor, then? said Grif. "Can I tempt you with some of this?"

"Grif, I had forgot how revolting you are. Not unless you cook it first."

Later, he showed Grif the ring of Neap, and related how Methvet Nian had given it to him; told him of the events in Bread Street, and of the curious desertion of Carron Ban; and narrated his encounter with the lammergeyer in the Cruachan mist.

"And you have no desire to follow this bird?" asked Grif.

"Whatever Cellur of Lendalfoot may think, if Viricon goes down, everything else follows it. The defeat of the Moidart is my priority."

"Things have grown dark and fragmented," mused Grif. "We do not have all the pieces of the puzzle. I worry that we shall solve it too late for the answer to be of any use."

"Still: we must go up against the Moidart, however unprepared, and even though that would seem not to be the whole of it."

"Unquestionably," said Grif: "But think, Cromis: if the fall of Viriconium is but a part, then what is the shape or dimension of the whole? I have had dreams of immense ancient forces moving in darkness, and I am beginning to feel afraid."

The lammergeyer waddled forward from the fire, its wings opened a little way, and stared at the two men.

"Fear the *geteit chemosit*," it said. "*tegeus-Cromis*

of Viriconium should go at once to the tower of Cellur, which—"

"Go away and peck your feathers, bird," said Grif. "Maybe you'll find steel lice there." To Cromis, he suggested: "If you have eaten enough, we'll go into the town. A search of the taverns may yet bring Trinor to light."

They walked the short distance to Duirinish by the banks of the Minfolin, each occupied by his own thoughts. A low white mist, hardly chest high, covered the Leedale, but the sky was clear and hard. The Name Stars burned with a chilly emerald fire: for millennia they had hung there, spelling two words in a forgotten language; now, only night-herders puzzled over their meaning.

At the steel gates, their way was barred by guards in mail shirts and low, conical helmets, who looked suspiciously at Grif's gaudy clothes and the huge bird that perched on Cromis' arm. Their officer stepped forward and said:

"No one enters the city after dark." His face was lined with responsibility, his voice curt. "We are bothered constantly by northmen and spies. You had best wait until the morning." He studied Grif. *"If* you have legitimate business."

Birkin Grif stared unkindly at him, and then slowly up at the great black sweep of the walls. From far above came the faint ring of footsteps on stone.

"So," he said. "It's either climb that lot, or break your pompous face. The latter seems to me the easier." He flexed his hands suggestively. "Let us in, stupid."

"Hold off, Grif," said Cromis, restraining him. "It's a wise precaution. They are merely doing their job."

He held his hands well away from the hilt of the nameless sword and advanced. He slid the ring of Neap from his finger and held it out for the officer's inspection. "That is my authority. I will take responsibility for your opening the gate, should any question arise. I am on the Queen's business."

He took back the ring, returned the officer's short bow, and they passed into the Stone City.

Inside, the roads were narrow, to facilitate defense, should the gate be taken or the outer walls breached. The gloomy granite buildings—for the main part barracks and weaponaries and storehouses—huddled together, their second storeys hanging out over the streets so that fire could be poured into an invader from above. Their windows were morose slits. Even in the commercial center, where the houses of the metal and fur trade stood, the buildings had an air of dour watchfulness. Duirinish had never been a gay city.

"The army passed through here some days ago," said Grif. "They must have had a fairly glum time of it."

"More important," Cromis told him, "is that they must be well on their way to Ruined Glenluce by now, even travelling by the old coastal road."

"We'll catch them by going directly north. Straight through the Marshes, fast and light across the Rust Desert. Not a pleasant trip, but speedy."

"If the Moidart catches them on that road before Glenluce, the fight will be over before we find it," Cromis muttered, brooding on that thought.

They spent an hour traveling the narrow ways that spiraled up toward Alves, stopping at two inns. There, they found no sign of Norvin Trinor, and fellow-customers tended to avoid Cromis and his bird. But in the Blue Metal Discovery, a place in the commercial quarter, they came upon another Methven.

A three-story inn built for the convenience of the fatter merchant classes, the Blue Metal Discovery took up one entire side of Replica Square, less than a mile from Alves itself. Its façade was lit by soft and expensive blue lights salvaged many years before from the Rust Desert; and its windows were less forbidding than the majority in the town, having white ornamental iron shutters reminiscent of those found on dwellings in the warmer parts of the South.

By the time they came to Replica Square, Birkin Grif seemed to be having some trouble in placing his feet squarely on the cobbles. He walked very carefully, singing loudly and continuously a verse of some maudlin Cladich lament. Even to Cromis things looked a little less somber. No change of mood was discernible in the bird.

The doors of the inn were wide open, spilling yellow light into the blue and a great racket into the quiet square. One or two customers emerged hurriedly from the place and walked off looking furtively behind them. Shouts mingled with the sound of moving furniture. Birkin Grif stopped singing and swaying and became quite still. A little introspective smile crossed his jowly features.

"That," he said, "is a *fight*." And he hurried off, his stride abruptly sure and steady.

He was halfway across the square before Cromis came up with him. They stood in the wash of light from the open door and gazed into a long room.

At its near end, behind a cluster of overturned trestle-tables, huddled two potboys and some wanlooking customers, shifting their feet nervously in a mess of sawdust and spilt food. The innkeeper, plump, red-faced and perspiring, had poked his head into the room through a serving hatch; he was banking a heavy metal mug repeatedly on its sill and shouting abuse at a group of figures in the center of the room by the massive stone fireplace.

There were seven of them: five heavily-built men with wiry black hair and beards, dressed in the brown leather leggings and coats of metal-scavengers; a serving girl in the blue shift of the house (she was crushed into the chimneybreast, her hand to her mouth, and her grimy face was fearful); and an old man in a ribbed and padded doublet of russet velvet.

All six men had drawn swords, and the graybeard, his whiskers wine-stained about the mouth, held also the wicked stump of a broken bottle. He was snarling, and they were advancing on him.

"*Theomeris Glyn!*" bellowed Grif. The metal-scavengers halted their confident advance and turned to stare warily at him. The landlord ceased his swearing, and his eyes bulged.

"You *silly* old goat! You should be passing your remaining years in decent contemplation; not bickering over dirty-girls—"

Theomeris Glyn looked a little embarrassed. "Oh, hello," he said. His gray eyes glittered shiftily above his hooked, red-veined nose. He peered at Grif. "I'm trying to catch up with the army," he muttered defensively. "They left me behind." His face brightened, thick white eyebrows shooting up into his tangled hair. "Heh, heh. Come and stamp some lice, eh, Grif? Now you're here?"

He cackled, and feinted suddenly toward his nearest opponent with the broken bottle. Breath hissed and feet shuffled in the sawdust. Old he may have been, but he was still viperishly quick: bright blood showed where his sword had made the true stroke, and the man danced back, cursing.

His companions closed in.

Grif hurled himself ungracefully across the floor to forestall them, dragging at his sword. But Cromis held back, wondering what to do with the lammergeyer. It gazed beadily at him.

"To ensure your safety," it said, "I suggest you leave here immediately. It is unwise to risk yourself in a minor combat. Cellur has need of you."

Whereupon it launched itself from his arm, screaming and beating its great gray wings like a visitation from Hell. Astonished, he watched it tear with three-inch talons at a white and shouting face (this was too much for the fat innkeeper; wailing with horror as the bird tore at its victim, he slammed the serving hatch shut and fled). Cromis drew sword, marked his man. He saw Grif wade in, cutting out right and left, but had no time to watch: a dull blade with a notched edge slashed in high at his skull.

He ducked, crouched, and thrust his sword up with both hands into his assailant's groin. With a terrible cry, the man dropped his weapon and fell over backwards, clutching at himself.

Cromis jumped over his writhing body as a second scavenger came howling at him from behind. He landed in an acrobatic crouch, rolled away. The room became a tumbling blur full of screams and the beating of giant wings.

(In the fireplace, Theomeris Glyn was shoving his enemy's head into the flames. He was a nasty old man. The fifth scavenger had backed up against the serving hatch, blood pouring down his face, and was pushing ineffectually at the screeching lammergeyer: Grif, who had already felled his first man, seemed to be trying to haul the bird off its prey so he could get in a clear swing.)

. . . Cromis moved easily behind a wild stroke. "Stop now, and you go unharmed," he panted. But his opponent spat, and engaged the nameless sword.

"I'll *stick* yer!" he hissed.

Cromis slid his steel down the man's blade, so that they locked hilts. His free hand went unseen beneath his cloak; then, deliberately releasing his pressure on the locked swords, he fell forward. For a moment, their bodies touched. He slid the *baan* into the scavenger's heart, and let the body fall.

His knuckles had been cut and bruised as the swords disengaged; he licked them absently, staring at the corpse. A steel medallion showed at its throat. He felt a touch on his shoulder.

"That last was a pretty filthy trick," said Grif, smiling a queer, strained smile. "You must teach me some time."

"You're too heavy on your feet. And I'd rather teach you to sing. Look at this—"

He poked with the tip of his sword at the scavenger's medallion. It glinted in the bright light. It was a coin, but not of Viriconium: in high relief, it bore the arms of Canna Moidart: wolf's head beneath three towers.

"Already she prepares to rule," said Cromis. "These were Northerners. We must leave at first light. I fear we shall arrive too late."

As he spoke, shouting and commotion broke out again behind them.

In the fireplace, Theomeris Glyn of Soubridge, the old campaigner, was struggling with the serving girl. Her blue bodice had come awry, but she had placed four neat welts on his left cheek. Her small grubby fists hammered on him.

"A man who may not survive his Queen's wars *needs* a little affection!" he cried petulantly. "Oh *drat!*"

Behind him stood the landlord, wringing greasy hands over the wreckage and demanding payment of his bony, oblivious shoulders.

Birkin Grif wheezed and chuckled. Cromis could raise only a thin, weary smile: he had been much disturbed by his discovery.

"Go and pull the old fool off her, Grif, and we'll take him with us. At least he'll see action again, for what it's worth."

Later, as they passed the gates of Duirinish, old Glyn dawdling drunkenly behind them, Grif said:

"She prepares her way to rule, as you say. Her confidence is immense. What can half a hundred brigands, a poet and an ancient lecher do to flex a will such as that?"

4

Next morning, in the thin light of dawn, Grif's company wound past the dark, watchful walls of the Stony City and into the North. Rivermist rose fading up toward the sun in slender spires and pillars. Duirinish was silent but for the tramping of guards on the high battlements. A heron perched on a rotting log to watch as the tiny force forded the northern meander of the Minfolin. If it found them curious, it gave no sign, but flapped heavily away as the white spray flew from cantering hooves.

They had abandoned their ragged, weather-stained finery for makeshift war-gear. Here and there, mail rings winked, and some of them wore odd bits of plate-armor; but for the most part, it was steel-studded leather stuff. They were a grim, rough-handed crew, with wind-burnt faces and hard, hooded eyes: their speech was harsh, their laughter dangerous, but their weapons were bright and well-kept, and the coats of their mounts gleamed with health over hard muscle.

Birkin Grif rode with wry pride at their head.

His massive frame was clad in mail lacquered cobalt-blue, and he wore over that a silk tabard of the same acid yellow as his mare's caparisons. He had relinquished his rustic hat, and his mane of blond hair blew back in the light wind. At his side was a great broadsword with a silver-bound hilt; in a scabbard hanging from his saddle-bow rested his long-axe, to hand in case he should be unhorsed. The roan mare arched her powerful neck, shook her big, beautiful head. Her bridle was of soft red leather with a subtle copper filigree inlaid.

To Cromis, riding beside him hunched against the chill on a somber black gelding, wrapped in his dark cloak like a raven in its feathers, it seemed that Grif and his horse threw back the hesitant morning light like a challenge: for a moment, they were heraldic and invincible, the doom to which they traveled something beautiful and unguessed. But the emotion was brief and passed, and his moroseness returned.

At Birkin Grif's left, his seat insecure on a scruffy pack-horse, Theomeric Glyn, his only armor a steel-stressed leather cap, grumbled at the cold and the earliness of the hour, and cursed the flint hearts of city girls. And behind the three Methven, Grif's men had begun to chant a rhythmic Rivermouth song of forgotten meaning, *The Dead Freight Dirge*:

> Burn them up and sow them deep:
>   Oh, *Drive them down;*
> Heavy weather in the Fleet:
>   Oh, *Drive them down;*
> Gather them up and drive them down:

Oh, *Sow them deep;*
Withering wind and plodding feet:
Oh, *Drive them down!*

Its effect on Cromis was hypnotic: as the syllables rolled, he found himself sinking into a reverie of death and spoliation, haunted by gray, translucent images of a shattered Viriconium. The face of Methvet Nian hung before him, in the grip of some deep but undefinable sorrow. He knew he could not go to her. He was aware of the metal bird of Cellur, gyring and hovering high above him as he rode, the embodiment of a threat he could not name.

He was sinking deeper, like a man in a drug-dream, when Grif reined in his mare and called his men to a halt.

"Here we leave the Old North Road," he said. "There's our way; direct but unpleasant."

Before them, the road turned abruptly West and was lost to sight behind the black terminal massif of Low Leedale Edge: from there, it found its way to the coast and began the long journey North.

But straight ahead among the bracken and coarse grass at the mouth of the valley ran a narrow track. Fifty yards from the road, the heather failed, and the terrain became brown, faintly iridescent bog streaked with slicks of purple and oily yellow. Beyond that rose thickets of strangely shaped trees. The river meandered through it, slow and broad, flanked by dense reedbeds of a bright ocher color. The wind blew from the North, carrying a bitter, metallic smell.

"The Metal-salt Marshes," murmured Grif. He pointed to the reedbeds by the Minfolin. "Even in Winter the colors are weird. In Summer, they bemuse

58

the brain. The birds and insects there are peculiar, too."

"Some might find it beautiful," said Cromis; and he did.

Theomeris Glyn snorted. He pinched his beaky nose. "It *stinks*," he said. "I wish I hadn't come. I am an old man and deserve better."

Grif smiled.

"This is just the periphery, graybeard. Wait until we reach the interior, and the water-thickets."

Where the valley bracken petered out, a dyke had been sunk to prevent the herd-animals of Low Leedale from wandering into the bog. It was deep and steep-sided, full of stagnant water over which lay a multicolored film of scum. They crossed it by a gated wooden bridge, the hooves of their horses clattering hollowly. Above them, Cellur's lammergeyer was a black speck in the pale blue unclouded sky.

In the water-thickets, the path wound tortuously between umber iron-bogs, albescent quicksands of aluminium and magnesium oxides, and sumps of cuprous blue or permanganate mauve fed by slow, gelid streams and fringed by silver reeds and tall black grasses. The twisted, smooth-barked boles of the trees were yellow-ocher and burnt orange; through their tightly woven foliage filtered a gloomy, tinted light. At their roots grew great clumps of multifaceted translucent crystal like alien fungi.

Charcoal gray frogs with viridescent eyes croaked as the column floundered between the pools. Beneath the greasy surface of the water unidentifiable reptiles moved slowly and sinuously. Dragonflies whose webby wings spanned a foot or more hummed and hovered between the sedges: their long, wicked bodies glittered bold green and ultramarine; they took their prey on the wing, pouncing with an audible snap of jaws on whining, ephemeral mosquitoes and fluttering moths of april blue and chevrolet cerise.

Over everything hung the heavy, oppressive stench of rotting metal. After an hour, Cromis' mouth was coated with a bitter deposit, and he tasted acids. He found it difficult to speak. While his horse stumbled and slithered beneath him, he gazed about in wonder, and poetry moved in his skull, swift as the jeweled mosquito-hawks over a dark slow current of ancient decay.

Grif drove his men hard, aiming to traverse the marsh in three days: but their beasts were reluctant, confused by prussian blue streams and fragile, organic pink sky. Some refused to move, bracing their legs and trembling, and had to be driven. They turned rolling white eyes on their owners, who cursed and sank to their boot-tops in the mud, releasing huge bubbles of acrid gas.

When they emerged from the trees for a short while at about noon, Cromis noticed that the true sky was full of racing, wind-torn gray clouds; and despite its exotic colors, the Metal-salt Marsh was cold.

In the evening of the third day, they reached the shallow waters of Cobaltmere in the Northern reaches of the marsh. They had lost two men and a horse to the shifting sands; a third man had died painfully after drinking from a deceptively clear pool, his limbs swelling up and turning silver-gray. They were tired and filthy, but pleased with the speed of their progress.

They made camp in a fairly dry clearing halfway round the waterlogged ambit of the mere. Far out on the water lay fawn mudbanks streaked with sudden yellow, and floating islands of matted vegetation on which waterbirds cackled, ruffling their electric-blue feathers. As the day decayed, the colors were numbed: but in the funereal light of sunset, the water of Cobaltmere came alive with mile-long stains of cochineal and mazarine.

Cromis was woken some time before dawn by what he assumed to be the cold. A dim, disturbing phosphorescence of fluctuating color hung over the mere and its environs; caused by some strange quality of the water there, it gave an even but wan light. There were no shadows. The dripping trees loomed vaguely at the periphery of the clearing.

When he found it impossible to sleep again, he moved nearer to the dead embers of the fire. He lay there uneasily, wrapped in blanket and cloak, his fingers laced beneath his head, staring up at the faint Name Stars.

About him humped the gray forms of sleeping men. Horses shifted drowsily behind him. A nocturnal mosquito-hawk with huge obsidian globes for eyes hunted over the shallows, humming and snapping. He watched it for a moment, fascinated. He could hear the wheeze of Theomeris Glyn's breathing, and the low sound of water draining through the reed-clumps. Grif had set a guard on the clearing: he moved slowly round its edge and out of Cromis' field of vision, blowing warmth into his cupped hands, his feet sinking with soft noises into the dank earth.

Cromis closed his eyes and wondered morosely if they would get clear of the marsh by the end of the next day. He discussed strategies suitable for the various areas in which they might meet the Moidart's host. He thought of Methvet Nian as he had last seen her, in the room with five windows that showed landscapes to be found nowhere in the kingdom.

He was considering the fine, firm set of her mouth when he heard a faint sigh behind him: not close, and too low-pitched to wake a sleeping man, but of quite peculiar strength and urgency.

Calmly, waiting for a moment of fear to pass, he felt for the hilt of the nameless sword. Finding it, he rolled cautiously on to his stomach, making as little unnecessary movement as possible and breathing silently through his open mouth. This maneuver brought into view the semicircle of clearing previously invisible to him. Stone-still, he studied the point from which the sigh had come.

He could discern little other than the vague, bent outlines of trees. A darker place marked the entrance to the glade. But there seemed to be nothing threatening there. The horses were quiet black silhouettes issuing a white mist of breath. One or two of them had cocked their ears forward alertly.

He realized that he could neither see nor hear the perimeter guard.

Carefully, he freed himself from his blankets, eased his sword a few inches from its scabbard. Reflex impelled him to crouch low as he ran across the clearing, and to change direction several times in case he had been marked by archers or energy-weapons. He felt exposed, but had no actual fear until he encountered the corpse of the guard.

It was lying near the gap in the trees: a huddled, ungainly form that had already sunk slightly into the wet ground. Upon closer examination, he found that the man had not even drawn his weapon. There was no blood apparent, and the limbs were uncut.

Kneeling, he grasped the cold, bearded jaw, his skin crawling with revulsion, and moved the head to ascertain whether the neck was broken. It was not. The skull, then. He probed reluctantly. Breath hissing through his clenched teeth, he leapt hurriedly to his feet.

The top of the man's skull was missing, sliced cleanly off an inch above the ears.

He wiped the mess off his fingers on some spongy grass, swallowing bile. Anger and fear flooded through him, and he shivered a little. The night was silent but for the far-off drowsy humming of a dragonfly. The earth round the body had been poached and churned. Big, shapeless impressions led away from it and out of the glade to the South. What sort of thing had made them, he could not tell. He began to follow them.

He had no thought of alerting the rest of the camp. He wanted vengeance for this pitiful, furtive death in a filthy place. It was a personal thing with him.

Away from Cobaltmere, the phosphorescence grew progressively dimmer; but his night-vision was good, and he followed the tracks swiftly. They left the path at a place where the trees were underlit by lumps of pale blue luminous crystal. Bathed in the unsteady glow, he stopped and strained his ears. Nothing but the sound of water. It occurred to him that he was alone. The ground sucked at his feet; the trees were weird, their boughs a frozen writhing motion. To his left, a branch snapped.

He whirled and threw himself into the undergrowth, hacking out with his sword. Foliage clutched at his limbs; at each step he sank into the muck; small animals scuttled away from him, invisible. He halted, breathing heavily, in a tiny clearing with a stinking pool. He could hear nothing. After a minute, he became convinced that he had been lured from the path; and in revealing himself to whatever moved so silently in the darkness he had lost his advantage. His skin crawled.

Only his peculiar defensive skills saved him. There was a baleful hissing behind him: he allowed his knees to buckle, and a cold green blade cut the air above his head; poised on his bent left leg, he spun himself round like a top, his sword slashing a half-circle at the knees of his assailant. Knowing that the stroke could not connect, he leapt back.

Before him loomed a great black shadow, some seven or eight feet high. Its limbs were thick and heavy, its head a blunted ovoid, featureless but for three glowing yellow points set in an isosceles triangle. It continued to hiss, its movements silky and powerful and controlled, leaving those strange, shapeless imprints in the mud beneath it. There was an alien coldness about it, a calm, calculating intelligence.

The great *baan*, that he did not dare meet with mere steel, cut a second arc toward him. He danced back, and it sliced through his mail shirt like a fingernail through cold grease; blood from a shallow wound warmed his chest. Despite its size, the thing was cruelly swift. He went behind its stroke, cutting over-hand at the place where its neck met shoulder: but it writhed away, and they faced one another again. Cromis had measured its speed, and feared he was outclassed.

There was no further sparring. In the dark place by the stinking pool, they went at it, and *baan* and steel performed a deadly, flickering choreography. And always Cromis must evade, hoping for a moment's carelessness: yet the shadow was as fast as he, and fought tirelessly. It forced him slowly to the lip of the pool, and a mist was in front of his eyes. He was cut in a number of places. His mail shirt hung in ribbons.

His heel touched water, and for an instant he allowed the *baan* to catch his blade. In a shower of sparks, the tip of the nameless sword was severed: now he could not thrust, but must use only its edge. Fear crept and coiled in him. The giant, its cluster of eyes pale and empty, loomed above him, chopping and leaping like an automaton. Abruptly, he saw a dangerous remedy.

Beneath his clothing, his right hand found the hilt of the little *baan* that had killed his sister. Clutching it, he feigned an injury, delaying a counterstroke and fumbling his recovery. He felt little hope for the stratagem. But the giant saw the opening: and as its weapon moved back, then down, Cromis whipped out the energy-knife and met with it the killing-blow.

There was terrifying flash as the two *baans* engaged and shorted out. Cromis was hurled bodily into the pool by the concussion of ancient energies, his arm paralyzed. Its blade dead and useless, the giant reeled drunkenly about the clearing, hissing balefully.

Cromis dragged himself from the water, arm numb with agony. Gagging and retching on the liquid that had entered his mouth, he renewed his attack; and found that in the final flurry of blades, the nameless sword had been cut cleanly in two halfway down its length. Cursing bitterly, he lashed out with the stump. But the giant turned and ran awkwardly into the trees, lumbering through the pool in a fountain of spray.

Its murderous confidence had been dispelled, its

grace had left it, and it was defeated: but Cromis cast himself on the poached earth and wept with pain and frustration.

Shouting broke out near him. On gray wings, Cellur's lammergeyer crashed through the foliage, flapping evilly across the clearing, and, screaming, sped after the fleeing shadow. Cromis felt himself lifted.

"Grif," he muttered. "My blade is broken. It was not a man. I injured it with a trick of Tomb's. There is ancients' work here—

"The Moidart has woken something we cannot handle. It almost took me."

A new fear settled like ice in his bone-marrow. He clutched desperately at the fingers of his left hand. "Grif, I could not *kill* it!

"And I have lost the Tenth Ring of Neap."

Despair carried him down into darkness.

Dawn broke yellow and black like an omen over the Cobalt-mere, where isolated wreaths of night-mist still hung over the dark, smooth water. From the eyots and reed-beds, fowl cackled: dimly sensing the coming winter, they were gathering in great multicolored drifts on the surface of the lake, slow migratory urges building to a climax in ten thousand small, dreary skulls.

"And there will be killing weather this year," murmured tegeus-Cromis, as he huddled over the fire gazing at the noisy flocks, his sword in three pieces beside him, the shreds and tatters of his mail-coat rattling together as he moved. They had treated his numerous cuts and bruises, but could do nothing for the state of his thoughts. He shuddered, equating the iron

66

earths of winter with lands in the North and the bale in the eyes of hunting wolves.

He had woken from a brief sleep, his mouth tasting of failure, to find Grif's men straggling back in despondent twos and threes from a search of the glade where he had met the dark giant; and they reported that the Tenth Ring of Neap was gone without trace, trodden deep into the churned mud, or sunk, perhaps, in the fetid pool. That metal bird, too, had returned to him, having lost its quarry among the water-thickets. Now he sat with Theomeris Glyn, who had snored like a drunk through all the chaos.

"You take single setback too hard," said the old man, sucking bits of food from his whiskers. He was holding a strip of meat to the flames with the tip of his knife. "You'll learn—" He sniggered, nodding his head over the defeats of the aged. "Still, it is strange.

"It was always said South of the Pastel City that if tegeus-Cromis and the nameless sword could not kill it, then it must already be dead. Strange. Have some cooked pig?"

Cromis laughed dully. "You are small comfort. An old man mumbling over meat and homilies. What shall we do without the Queen's Authorization? What *can* we do?"

Birkin Grif came up to warm his hands over the fire. He sniffed at the cooking meat like a fat bloodhound, squeezed his great bulk carefully into the space between Cromis and the old man.

"Only what we would have done had we kept the thing," he said. "Manufacture dooms in your head and you will go mad. Reality is incontrovertible. Also, it will not be anticipated."

"But to command an army—" began Cromis helplessly.

Grif scraped half-heartedly at the filth on his boots. "I have seen you command before, poet. It appeared to me then that you did so from the strengths of your own self, not from those of some bauble."

"That's true," Old Glyn said judiciously, spitting out some gristle. "That's how we did it in the old days. Damned expensive boots, those, Grif. You ought to saddle-soap them to keep the damp out. Not that I ever commandeered anything but the arse of a wench."

Grif clasped Cromis' shoulder, shook it gently. "Brooder, it was *not* your fault."

Cromis shrugged. It made him feel no better. "You buried the guard?" he asked, hoping to change the subject.

Grif's smile vanished. He nodded. "Aye, and found one more piece for the puzzle. I was fascinated by the precise edge of his wound. Examining it more closely, I found—" He paused, prodded the fire with his boot and watched the ascending sparks. "We buried only a part of that man, Cromis: the rest has gone with the creature you put to flight.

"His brain has been stolen."

There was a silence. The colorful trees dripped. Theomeris Glyn began to chew noisily. Cromis reached out to toy with the shards of his sword, unpleasant visions of the corpse crawling through his head: the huddled limbs in the mud, the congealing broth at the edge of the wound.

He said: "She has woken something from the Old Science. I am sorry for that man, and I see each of us in him—" He slid the shards of the nameless sword one by one into his scabbard. "We are all dead men, Grif." He stood up, his muscles aching from the long night. "I'll make ready my horse. We had best to move on."

Perched on an overhanging bough with pale turquoise bark, the metal lammergeyer eyed him silently.

"Sure you won't have some pig—?" offered Theomeris Glyn.

They reached the northerly bounds of the marsh without further loss of men. By afternoon on the fourth day the gaudy foliage had thinned sufficiently to reveal a sky overcast but of more acceptable color. Their speed increased as the going firmed steadily. The bog broke up into irregular patches separated by wide, flat causeways, tending to the color of rust as as they moved north. A cold wind billowed their cloaks, plucked at Cromis' torn mail, and fine rain dulled the hides of the horses.

Stretching east and west in a great lazy curve, the terminal barrens of the Great Brown Waste barred their way: chains of dun-colored dunes interconnecting to form a low scarp, the face of which was cut and seamed by massive gully erosion.

"We are lucky to come here in winter," said Birkin Grif, twisting in his saddle as he led the company in single file up the gently-sloping cleft worn by a black and gelid stream. Walls of damp russet loess reared lifelessly on either side. "Although the winds are stronger, they carry more moisture to lay the soil. The Waste is not a true desert."

Cromis nodded dully. In the Low Leedale it had been autumn yet, but that was hard to believe here. He fixed his eyes on the narrow strip of sky beyond the lips of the ravine, wishing for Balmacara, where the year died more happily.

"There is slightly less danger of earth-falls, you

understand, and clouds of dust. In summer, one might choke to death, even here on the edge."

From the uncomfortable sky, Cromis shifted his gaze to the file of men behind him. They were lost in a mist of rain, dim shapes huddled and silent on tired mounts.

At the top of the gully, the entire company halted, and by common, unspoken consent, fanned out along the crest of a dune: each man held solitary and introspective by the bleak panorama before him.

The Waste rolled north—umber and ocher, dead, endless. Intersecting streams with high, vertical banks scored deep, meaningless ideographs in the earth. In the distance, distorted into deceptive, organic forms, metal girders poked accusing fingers at the empty air, as if there the Rust Desert might fix the source of its millennial pain. Grif's smugglers muttered, and found that a narrowed eye might discern certain slow but definite movements among the baffling curves of the landscape.

But tegeus-Cromis turned his horse to face away from the spoiled land, and stared back at the mauve haze that marked the marshes. He was much preoccupied by giants.

5

"We should not strive too hard to imitate the Afternoon Cultures," said Grif. "They killed this place with industry and left it for the big monitors. In part, if not in whole, they fell because they exhausted the land. We mine the metal they once used, for instance, because there is no ore left in the earth.

"And in using it all up, they dictated that our achievements should be of a different quality to theirs—"

"There will be no more Name Stars," murmured Cromis, looking up from the fragments of his sword. Dusk had drawn a brown veil across the wastes, amplifying the peculiar vagueness of the dune landscape. It was cold. As yet, they had seen no lizards: merely the slow, indistinct movements among the dunes that indicated their presence.

"Or any more of *this*," said Grif, bleakly.

71

They had made camp amid the ruins of a single vast, roofless building of vanished purpose and complicated ground-plan. Although nine tenths of it had sunk long ago beneath the bitter earth, the remains that reared around them rose fifty or sixty feet into the twilight. A feeble wind mumbled in off the Waste and mourned over their indistinct summits. Among the dunes meandered a vile, sour watercourse, choked with stones worn and scoured by Time.

Two or three fires burned in the lee of a broken load-wall. Grif's men tended them silently. Infected by the bleakness of the Waste, they had picketed the horses close, and the perimeter guards kept well within sight of the main body.

"There will be no more of anything soon," said Theomeris Glyn. "The Moidart, the Afternoon Cultures—both are Time by another name. You are sentimentalists, lacing a proper sense of perspective. When you get to my age—"

"We will grow bored and boring, and make fools of ourselves with dirty girls in Duirinish. It will be a fine time, that."

"You may not make it that far, Birkin Grif," said the old man darkly.

Since Cromis' fight in the Metal-salt Marsh, Cellur's mechanical vulture had spent most of its time in the air, wheeling in great slow circles over the Waste. It would report nothing it had seen from that vantage. Now it perched just beyond the circle of firelight and said:

"Post-industrial shock effected by the so-called 'Afternoon Cultures' was limited in these latitudes. There is evidence, however, that to the west there exists an entire continent despoiled to the degree of the Great Brown Waste.

"In a global sense, the old man may be right: we are running out of Time."

Its precise reedy voice lent a further chill to the night. In the silence that followed, the wind aged, the dying sun ran down like clockwork in an orrery. Birkin Grif laughed uncomfortably; a few thin echoes came from his men.

"Bird, *you* will end up as rust, with nothing to your credit but unproven hypotheses. If we are at the end of Time, what have you to show for it? Are you, perhaps, jealous that you cannot experience the misery of flesh, which is this: to know intimately the doom *you* merely parrot, and yet die in hope?"

The bird waddled forward, firelight spraying off its folded wings.

"That is not given to me," it said. "It will not be given to you, if you fail the real task implicit in this war: *fear the geteit chemosit; travel at once to the tower of Cellur, which you will find—*"

Filled with a horrible depression, Cromis dropped the shards of his sword and left the fire. From his saddlebag he took his curious eastern instrument. He bit his lip and wandered past the picket line and the perimeter guards. With death in his head, he sat on a stone. Before him, huge loops of sand-polished girder dipped in and out of the dunes like metal worms. They are frozen, he thought: Caught on a strange journey across an alien planet at the forgotten end of the universe.

Shivering, he composed this:

Rust in our eyes . . . metallic perspective trammel us in the rare earth north . . . we are nothing but eroded men . . . wind clothing our eyes with white ice . . . we are the swarf-eaters . . .

hardened by our addiction, tasting acids. . . . Little to dream here, our fantasies are iron and icy echoes of bone . . . rust in our eyes, we who had once soft faces.

"Rust in our eyes—" he began again, preparing to repeat the chant in the Girvanian Mode: but a great shout from the camp drove it out of his skull. He jumped to his feet.

He saw the metal bird explode into the air, shedding light like a gunpowder rocket, its wings booming. Men were running about the encampment, casting febrile shadows on the ancient walls. He made pitiful grabbing motions at his empty scabbard, hurrying toward the uproar. Over a confusion of voices he heard Grif bellow suddenly:

"Leave it alone! Oh, you stupid pigs, leave it alone!"

Obsessed by his fantasies of an alien world, Cromis was for a moment unable to identify the dark, massive shape fidgeting and grunting in the gloom of the dead building. Drawn out of the inhospitable dunes by the warmth or the light and surrounded by men with swords, it seemed to be mesmerized and bemused by the fire—a lean, heavy body slung low between queerly-articulated legs, a twenty foot denizen of his own imagination.

He was almost disappointed to recognize it as one of the black reptiles of the Waste, huge but harmless, endowed by the folk-lore of Viriconium with the ability to eat metal.

"Big lizard," muttered one of Grif's brigands, with sullen awe: "Big lizard."

Cromis found himself fascinated by the flat, squat head with its wicked undershot lower jaw and rudimentary third eye. He could discern none of the spines and baroque crests traditional in illustrations of the beast, simply a rough hide with a matt, non-reflective quality.

"Pull back," ordered Grif, quietly.

The men obeyed, keeping their weapons up. Left to itself, the reptile closed determinedly on the fire: finally, the flames leapt, perfectly reflected, in each of its eyes. There it stood for some minutes, quite still.

It blinked. Cromis suspected that whatever sluggish metabolic desires the fire had aroused were unfulfilled. Laboriously, it backed away. It shuffled back into the night, moving its head slowly from side to side.

As his men turned to follow, Grif said sharply, "I told you *no*. Just leave it be. It has harmed nothing." He sat down.

"We don't belong here any more," he said.

"What do you suppose it saw in there?" Cromis asked him.

Two days out into the barrens. It seemed longer.

"The landscape is so static," said Grif, "that Time is drawn out, and runs at a strange, slow speed."

"Scruffy metaphysics. You are simply dying of boredom. I think I am already dead." Old Theomeris slapped his pony's rump. "This is my punishment for an indiscreet life. I wish I had enjoyed it more."

Since noon that day they had been traveling through a range of low, conical slag hills, compelled by a surface of loose slate to lower their speed to a walk. The three-hundred-foot heaps of gray stone cast back hell-like echoes from the unsteady hooves of the horses. Landslips were frequent; limited, but unnerving.

Cromis took no part in the constant amiable bickering: it was as unproductive as the sterile shale. Further, he was concerned by the odd behavior of the lammergeyer.

Ten or fifteen minutes before, the bird had ceased flying its customary pattern of wide circles, and now hung in the air some eight hundred feet up, a silver cruciform slipping and banking occasionally to compensate for a thermal current rising from the slag tips. As far as he could tell, it was hovering above a point about a mile ahead of their present position and directly on their route.

"The bird has seen something," he said to Grif, when he was sure. "It is watching something. Call a halt and lend me a sword—no, not that great lump of iron, the horse will collapse beneath it—and I'll go and find out what it is."

It was queer, lonely excursion. For half an hour he worked along the precarious spiral paths, accompanied only by echoes. Desolation closed oppressively round him.

Once, the terrible, bitter silence of the slag hills was broken by a distant rhythmic tapping; a light, quick, mysterious ring of metal on metal: but a brief fall of rock drowned it out. It returned later as he was urging his horse down the last slope of the range, the Great Brown Waste spread once more before him, Cellur's metal vulture hanging like an omen five hundred feet above his head.

At the bottom of the slope, two horses were tethered.

A pile of dusty harness lay near them, and a few yards away stood a small red four-wheeled caravan of a type usually only seen south of Viriconium—traditionally used by the tinkers of Mingulay for carrying their large families and meager equipment. Redolent

of the temperate south, it brought to his mind images
of affectionate gypsy slatterns and their raucous children. Its big, thick-spoked wheels were picked out in
bright yellow; rococo designs in electric blue rioted
over its side panels; its curved roof was painted purple. Cromis was unable to locate the source of the tapping sound (which presently stopped), but a thin,
blue-gray spire of smoke was rising from behind the
caravan.

He realized that it was impossible to conceal his
presence from whoever was camped down there—his
horse's nervous, crabbing progress down the decline
was dislodging continuous slides of rock which
bounded away like live things—so he made no effort,
coming down as fast as possible, gripping his bor-
rowed sword tightly.

On the last five yards of the slope, momentum
overcame him: the horse's rear hooves slid from beneath it; it pecked; and he rolled out of the saddle
over its shoulder. He landed dazed and awkward in
the gritty, sterile sand of the Waste, and dropped his
sword. Fine, stinging particles of dust got into his
eyes. He stumbled to his feet, eyes blind and streaming, unpleasantly aware of his bad tactical position.

"Why don't you just stand there quietly," said a
voice he thought he knew, "and make no attempt to
regain that rather clumsy sword? Eh?" And then:
"You caused enough fuss and furor for ten men
coming down that hill."

Cromis opened his eyes.

Standing before him, a power-axe held in his
knotty, scarred hands, was a thin figure no more than
four feet high, with long white hair and amused, pale
gray eyes. His face was massively ugly—it had an
unformed look, a childlike, disproportionate caste to

77

its planes—and the teeth revealed by his horrible grin were brown and broken. He was dressed in the heavy leather leggings and jerkin of a metal-prospector, and standing on end the haft of his axe would have topped him by a foot.

"You," said Cromis, "could have done no better. You are as insubordinate as ever. You are a pirate. Put up that axe, or my familiar spirit—" Here, he pointed to the vulture spiraling above them "—will probably tear the eyes from your unfortunate face. I have a great deal of trouble in restraining it from such acts."

"You will, however, concede that I've captured you? I'll chop the bloody bird up for dogsmeat if you don't—"

And with that, Tomb the Dwarf, as nasty a midget as ever hacked the hands off a priest, did a little complicated shuffle of triumph round his victim, cackling and sniggering like a parrot.

"If I had known it was you," said Cromis, "I'd have brought an army of occupation, to keep you quiet."

Night.

A pall, a shroud, of darkness lay over the slag heaps, to cover decently their naked attitudes of geographical death. Out on the Waste, the harsh white glare of Tomb's portable furnace dominated the orange flickering of a circlet of cooking fires.

Underlit by a savage glow like a dawn in hell, the little Rivermouth man's unbelievable face became demoniac, bloodcurdling. His hammer fell in measured, deadly strokes on to the soft, hot steel, and, as he worked, he droned and hummed a variant of that queer *Dead Freight* dirge:

Burn them up and *drive* them deep;
Oh, drive them *down!*

It was Cromis' nameless sword, now whole, that
flared in the furnace and sparked on the anvil, and
drew closer to its gloomy destiny with every accentu-
ated syllable of the chant.

After the meeting by the caravan, Cromis had
called down the vulture and sent it to fetch Grif from
his position in the hills. On his arrival, he had bellowed like an ox: it was a wild reunion between him
and the Dwarf, the one bellowing with laughter and
the other capering and crowing. Now Grif was eating raw meat and shouting at his brigands, while
Tomb and Cromis worked the forge.

"You interrupted me," shouted the Dwarf over the
roar and wail of the bellows. "I was repairing that."

And he jerked his thumb at a tangle of curved,
connected silver-steel rods—resembling nothing so
much as the skeleton of some dead metal giant—
which lay by the furnace. Small versions of the motors
that powered the airboats were situated at the joints
of its limbs, and a curious arrangement of flexible
metal straps and stirrups was attached half way
down each of its thighbones and upper arms. It
looked like the ugly, purposeful work of long-dead
men, an inert but dangerous colossus.

"What is it?" asked Cromis.

"You'll see when we get a fight. I dug it up about
a month ago. They had some beautiful ideas, those
old scientists." The light of Tomb's sole enthusiasm
—or was it simply splashback from the furnace?—
burned in his eyes, and Cromis had to be content with
that.

Later, the four Methven sat round a fire with a jug

of distilled wine. The reforged sword was cooling, the furnace powered-down, the brigands noisily asleep or dozing in their smelly blankets.

"No," said Tomb, "we aren't too far behind them." He displayed his repugnant teeth. "I'd have been up with Waterbeck and his well-disciplined babes by now, but I wanted to get that power-armor in good order."

"It won't be the same as the old days," complained old Glyn. He had passed rapidly into the sodden, querulous phase of drunkenness. "Now *there* was a time."

Tomb chuckled. "Why did I saddle myself this way? A graybeard with a bad memory, a braggart, and a poet who can't even look after his own sword. I think I might join the other side." He leered down at his hands. "Time I killed somebody, really. I feel like killing something."

"You're a nasty little beast, aren't you?" said Birkin Grif. "Have some more wine."

Cromis, content to have found Tomb if not Norvin Trinor, smiled and said nothing. More roads than this lead to Ruined Glenluce, he thought.

But in the end they had no need to go as far as Glenluce, and Tomb's prediction proved true: two days later, they came upon Lord Waterbeck's expeditionary force, camped several miles south-east of that unfortunate city, in a spot where the Waste had heaved itself into a series of low ridges and dead valleys filled with the phantoms of the Departed Cultures. Time is erosion: an icy wind blew constant abrasive streams of dust over the bare rock of the ridge: it had been blowing for a thousand years.

His black cloak flapping about him, tegeus-Cromis gazed down on the ancient valley; at his side, Grif stamped his feet and blew into his cupped hands. Beneath them spread the tents and bothies of Waterbeck's army—multicolored, embroidered with sigils and armorial bearings, but hardly gay. Canvas whipped and cracked, the wind moaned in the guy-lines, and armor clattered as the message runners hurried to and fro between piles of gear that lay in apparent confusion around the encampment.

The tents radiated as a series of spokes—each one representing a division of foot or horse—from a central pavilion surrounded by a complex of ancillary bothies: Lord Waterbeck's command center. There, canvas was replaced by oiled scarlet silk, shot through with threads of gold wire.

"He has a fine sense of his own importance," said Grif scathingly. "We had better go down and upset it."

"You are too harsh. Don't prejudge him." Cromis felt no enthusiasm for the task ahead. He fingered the hilt of the reforged sword and tried to shrug off his reluctance. "Tell Tomb to settle your men well apart from the main body, while we do what we can."

They rode down one of the wide avenues between the tents, Grif resplendent on his yellow-caparisoned mare, Cromis crow-black in the cold, old wind. They drew a few stares from unoccupied footsoldiers, but, in general, interest was reserved for Grif's smugglers, who were setting up camp around Tomb's gaudy caravan. It was an unconscious parody of Waterbeck's deployment, with the wagon replacing his showy pavilion. They looked like a traveling road-show.

Cromis caught threads and tail-ends of conversation as he rode:

"The Moidart . . ."

". . . and you can't trust a rumor."

"Twenty *thousand* northmen . . ."

". . . the Moidart . . ."

". . . and bloody airboats. Bloody scores of them!"

"What can you do about it?"

". . . glad to get it over and done."

". . . the *Moidart.*"

At barely thirty years of age, Lord Waterbeck of
Faldich had imposing gray hair—cut short and
smoothed impeccably back from his forehead—and
an urbane manner. His features were bland and
boneless, his skin unwrinkled but of a curiously dry,
aged texture. He wore a neat, tight jacket of tasteful
brown cord, quite unadorned, as were his well-
shaped, unobtrusively-manicured hands. Cromis
imagined that it would be difficult for him to offend
any of his peers, and that it was precisely this inabil-
ity that had earned him his present position.

When they entered the pavilion (it was less opulent
than its outer appearance suggested, and draughty) he
was sitting behind a small, cluttered camp table, adding his signature to a sheet of white vellum covered
with careful gray script. He raised his head, nodded
brusquely, and gave his attention to his work again.

"There *is* an official recruitment booth just along
the way," he said, his voice crisp and pleasant. "But
never mind, now you're here. I'll call an orderly and
have him deal with you here."

He looked up and smiled very briefly.

"From your appearance, I'd say you've come some
distance to serve. Encouraging to see newcomers, although there won't be many more. Well done, men."

Birkin Grif stepped forward, simultaneously puzzled
and antagonistic. "This is Lord tegeus-Cromis of Viriconium," he said, "a knight of the Order of Methven.

We are here on the Queen's business. It is imperative that—"

"Just one moment, please."

Waterbeck consulted a small ledger, nodded to himself. He folded his dispatch and began to address it.

"Perhaps Lord Cromis would prefer to speak for himself, eh?"

He offered them his brief little smile.

"You understand that I have many things to occupy my time. Battle will be joined within a week, and fifteen thousand men out there rely on me. If you could—"

He made an apologetic gesture.

"I have been advised of no airboat landings recently. If you could give me the meat of your message now, perhaps we could discuss an answer later?"

"I am not a courier, Lord Waterbeck," said Cromis. "My purposes are military, and may be embarrassing to us both."

"I see. I've never run into you in the city, my lord. Our haunts must be different. Each man to his own, hm?"

He stood up and extended his right hand across the table, palm up.

"You will have some identification provided by Her Majesty, I take it?"

"I began my journey with such proofs," said Cromis, aware of how foolish he must sound. The man was giving him no help at all. "But due to a failure of my own, they were lost. However, the Queen will vouch for me. I suggest you dispatch an airboat to the—"

Waterbeck laughed. He sat down. He shook his head slowly.

"My dear man," he said. "My *dear* man. I might

be addressing a simple adventurer. Or even, though I am most reluctant to suggest it, a Northman. I cannot spare an airboat merely to check the credentials of every wanderer who comes in here with a mysterious —and unexplained—proposition.

"If you wish to *fight,* well then, I will sign you on; but I cannot even listen to whatever it is you propose without some concrete, immediate proof of your identity."

Birkin Grif scowled hideously. He leaned over the desk and put his face close to Waterbeck's. He hissed:

"You are a damned fool, or you would use different words to a Methven. At least listen to what we have to say. Lord Cromis led the sea-fight at Mingulay— and won it, too—before you were able to lift a practice sword—"

Waterbeck got to his feet.

"There is an official recruitment booth a few steps away from here," he said quietly. "I do not wish to hear any more of this."

Later, they sat on the tailboard of Tomb's caravan, watching the Dwarf as he made final adjustments to his peculiar device.

"He knew," said Grif. "He *knew* why we were there. He sensed it."

"You cannot tell that for sure. He was within his rights, if shortsighted. I did not have the ring, and even with that to ease the way it would have been a difficult meeting. He would have resented our command."

Grif made a chopping motion in the air, both hands locked together. He spat into a swirl of dust raised by the wind.

"He knew, all right. If he'd heard us out, he'd have been forced to dispatch that boat."

Tomb the Dwarf chuckled obscenely. He put down his tools and wiped his hands on the back of his leggings.

"Watch this here," he said. "When I've got this thing together, I'll visit Lord Waterbeck. I'll cut his onions off. I'll slice them thinly with my axe."

He had spread the immense skeleton on the ground, so that its legs stuck straight out and its arms were set close to its sides. Now, he lowered himself gently down until he lay supine on its cold bones.

He slid his feet into the stirrups on its thighs, and tightened the metal straps round his ankles. A complicated harness fastened his upper body into its ribcage.

"A cold embrace," he said.

He positioned his hands so as to reach certain levers that projected from the bones above its elbow-joint. Its jawless skull he hinged forward to fit over his head like a helmet. He lay there for a moment, strapped to the thing like a man crucified on a tree of insane design.

"I power it up now," he explained. He worked levers. A low, distinct humming filled the air. A smell of ozone reminded Cromis of the airboat disaster at Balmacara. "Ah," said Tomb. He manipulated studs and switches.

The skeleton twitched its huge steel bones.

Tomb sniggered.

He moved his arm, and a fleshless metal hand rose into the air. It made grasping motions. It flexed its fingers.

Tomb bent his legs, and came slowly to his feet. He was eleven feet tall.

"Where's my chopper?" he said. And, having found that weapon, he broke into a grotesque, capering dance, swinging it round his head in ecstatic but deadly figures of eight; lifting his new legs high to display them; pointing his nimble silver-steel toes.

"I'll *shorten* them!" he screamed, the wind whistling through his mechanical limbs. He ignored the helpless, delighted laughter of his friends. "I'll cut the sods!" He didn't say who. "Beautiful!" he crowed. And he stormed off, a gigantic paradox suspended on the thin line between comedy and horror, to test his machine by completing a full circuit of the encampment under the amazed eyes of fifteen thousand sensible fighting men.

Neither the Methven nor their tiny force of brigands ever signed up officially with Lord Waterbeck's army. His estimation of the Moidart's rate of progress toward Duirinish proved to be a little optimistic. An hour before dawn the next day, ten airboats bearing the sigil of the Wolf's Head and Three Towers howled over the northern ridge, their motors in overdrive.

Cromis was to be haunted for the rest of his life by his failure to understand how a general could become so concerned with the administration of his men and the politics of his war that he neglected the reports of his own reconnaissance corps.

6

Cromis was asleep when the attack began. In the soft, black space of his head a giant insect hovered and hummed, staring gloomily at him from human eyes, brushing the walls of his skull with its swift wings and unbearable, fragile legs. He did not understand its philosophy. The ideographs engraved on its thorax expressed a message of Time and the universe, which he learned by heart and immediately forgot. The whine of the wings deepened in pitch, and resolved itself into the monstrous wail of the Moidart's aircraft.

Birkin Grif was punching his shoulder repeatedly and yelling in his ear. He stumbled up, shaking the dream from his head. He saw Tomb the Dwarf scuttle out of the caravan, fling himself on to his exoskeleton and begin powering up. All around, men were shouting, pointing at the sky, their mouths like damp pits. The noise from Waterbeck's camp was tremendous; fifteen thousand simultaneous inarticulate cries of anger and fear.

He strapped on his sword. "We're too exposed!" They could do nothing about it. Long, fast shapes gyred above them, dim in the light of false dawn.

Evil red flares lit the valley as a section of the attacking squadron located Waterbeck's airboat park and began to bombard it with barrels of burning pitch and large stones. The remainder of the fleet separated and shrieked low over the encampment, dropping their loads at random to panic men and horses.

A detachment of Waterbeck's troops began firing one of the only three operative power-cannon that remained in the kingdom, its pale violet bolts flaming up like reversed bolide trails against a dark sky.

Grif harried his men. Between them, they regained control of the horses.

Despite the efforts of Waterbeck's own airboat men, two machines were destroyed—their spines broken, their ancient energies earthing away—before the rest of his meager wing hurled into the sky. The energy-cannon ceased firing immediately they were airborne, and the battle moved away from the ground.

Two boats, locked together and leaking strange pastel fireflies of released energy, drifted slowly over the encampment and vanished behind the southern ridge. Cromis shuddered: small dark shapes were falling from them, soundless and pathetic.

"Had I made a different choice, I might be up there now," murmured Tomb the Dwarf, looming up out of the red glare of the pitch fires. He sounded almost wistful.

"Cromis, there's something wrong with your vulture."

The bird was strutting to and fro on the roof of the caravan, where it had perched during the night. It extended its neck as if to vomit, beat its great iridium wings together, and squawked insanely. It made short, hopping sallies into the air. Suddenly, it shrieked:

"Go at once! Go at once! Go at once!"

It launched itself off the roof and fastened its talons on Cromis' arm. It bobbed its head, peered into his face.

"tegeus-Cromis, you should leave here at once and go to—"

But Cromis hardly heard. He was watching Canna Moidart's captains as they swarmed down the face of the northern ridge and into the valley—their standards raised high, thirty thousand Northmen at their backs, and the *geteit chemosit* coming on in dark waves before them.

Time bucked and whipped like a broken hawser in Cromis' head, and for a moment he existed at two separate and distinct points along its curve—

In a dark glade by a stinking pool, he fought a great black shadow some seven or eight feet high. Its limbs were thick and heavy, its head a blunted ovoid, featureless but for three glowing points set in an isosceles triangle. Its movements were powerful and controlled. It hissed as it wielded its enormous energy-blade, and left strange, shapeless imprints in the mud beneath it. There was an alien coldness about it; a calm, calculated intelligence—

Simultaneously, in the irrefutable present of the Great Brown Waste, he observed with unemotional preciseness the terrible skirmish-line that advanced into the valley ahead of the Moidart's horde. Each of its units was a great black shadow seven or eight feet high, wielding an immense energy-blade. Their movements were alien and silky and controlled, and the unpleasant triplex eyes glittered yellowly from blunt, ovoid heads—

"Beware the *geteit chemosit!*" cried the vulture on his arm.

Sick and shaking, he explored an understanding that had been open to him since his fight in the Metal-salt Marsh.

"I should have listened," he said. "We have no chance," he whispered.

"We have more than poor Waterbeck, perhaps," murmured Birkin Grif. He put a hand on Cromis' shoulder. "If we live, we will go to Lendalfoot and see the metal bird's owner. They are golems, automatic men, some filthy thing she has dug up from a dead city. He may know—"

"Nothing like this has been seen in the world for a thousand years," said Tomb the Dwarf. "Where did she *find* them?"

Unconcerned by such questions, Canna Moidart's black mechanical butchers moved implacably toward the first engagement in the War of the Two Queens: a war that was later to be seen as the mere opening battle of a wholly different—and greatly more tragic—conflict.

Their impact on Waterbeck's army was brutal. Already disorganized and disconcerted by the airboat raid, scattered, separated from their commanding officers, the Viriconese milled about their ruined encampment in a desperate and feeble attempt to form some sort of defensive position.

Faced by a human antagonist, they might have held their shaky line. Certainly, there burned in all of them a hatred of the Northman which might in other circumstances have overcome their tactical weakness and stiffened their resistance. But the *chemosit* slaughtered their self-possession.

They sobbed and died. They were hastily-conscripted, half-trained. Powered blades cut their swords like cheese. Their armor failed to armor them. They discovered that they did not belong there.

In the moment of first contact, a fine red mist sprayed up from the battleline, and the dying inhaled the substance of the dead while the living fought on in the fog, wondering why they had left their shops and their farms. Many of them simply died of shock and revulsion as the blood arced and spurted to impossible heights from the severed arteries of their fellows, and the air was filled with the stink of burst innards.

When the Moidart's regular troops joined the battle, they found little but confusion to check them. They howled with laughter and rattled their swords against their shields. They flanked Waterbeck's depleted force, split it into small, useless detachments, overran his pavilion, and tore him to pieces. They ringed the Viriconese and hammered them steadily against the grim anvil of the still-advancing *chemosit*. But there was resistance—

In the dead airboat park, someone managed to depress the barrel of the energy-cannon enough to fire it horizontally. For some seconds, its meteoric bolts—almost invisible in the daylight—hissed and spurted into the unbroken rank of the mechanical men. For a moment, it looked like discomfiting them; several burned like torches and then exploded, destroying others: but a small squad detached themselves from the main body, and, their power-blades chopping in unison, reached the gun with ease. It sputtered and went out, like a candle in the rain, and the gunners with it—

And, from a vantage-point on the roof of Tomb's caravan, Lord tegeus-Cromis of Viriconium, who imagined himself a better poet than swordsman, chose his moment. "They make their own underbelly soft. Their only strength lies in the *chemosit*." His head was full of death. The metal bird was on his arm. "To the south there, they are completely open." He turned to Birkin Grif. "We could kill a lot of them if your men were willing."

Grif unsheathed his sword and smiled. He jumped to the ground. He mounted his roan mare (in the gray light, her caparisons shone bravely) and faced his ugly, dishonest crew. "We will all die," he told them. He bared his teeth at them and they grinned back like foxes. "Well?"

They stropped their evil knives against their leather leggings. "What are we waiting for?" asked one of them.

"You bloody fools!" yelled Grif, and roared with laughter. "Nobody asked you to do this!"

They shouted and catcalled. They leapt into their saddles and slapped their knees in enjoyment of the joke. They were a gangrel, misfit lot.

Cromis nodded. He did not want to speak, but, "Thank you," he said to them. His voice was lost in the clangor of Waterbeck's defeat.

"I am already halfway there," chuckled Tomb the Dwarf. He adjusted some of his levers. He swung his axe a couple of times, just to be sure.

Theomeris Glyn sniffed. "An old man," he said, "deserves better. Why are we wasting time?" He looked a fool, and entirely vulnerable in his battered old helmet. He should have been in bed.

"Let's go then," said Cromis. He leapt down from the roof. He mounted up, the iridium vulture flapping above him. He drew the nameless sword. And with no battle cries at all, forty smugglers, three Methven and a giant dwarf hurled themselves into a lost fight. What else could they have done?

The dead and the half-dead lay in mounds, inextricably mixed. The ancient, unforgiving dust of the Great Brown Waste, recalling the crimes of the Departed Cultures, sucked greedily at these charnel heaps, and turned into mud. Some five thousand of Waterbeck's original force were still on their feet, concentrated in three or four groups, the largest of which had made its stand out of the bloody morass, on a long, low knoll at the center of the valley.

The momentum of the charge carried Cromis twenty yards into the press without the need to strike a blow: Northmen fell to the hooves and shoulders of his horse and were trampled. He shouted obscenities at them, and made for the knoll, the smugglers a flying wedge behind him. A pikeman tore a long strip of flesh from the neck of his mount; Cromis hung out of the saddle and swung for the carotid artery; blade bit, and splashed with the piker's gore the horse reared and screamed in triumph. Cromis hung on and cut about him, laughing. The stink of horse-sweat and leather and blood was as sharp as a knife.

To his left, Tomb the Dwarf towered above the Northmen in his exoskeleton, a deadly, glittering, giant insect, kicking in faces with bloodshod metal feet, striking terror and skulls with his horrible axe. On his right, Birkin Grif whirled his broadsword unscientifically about and sang, while murderous old Glyn taunted his opponents and stabbed them cunningly when they thought they had him. "We did things differently when I was your age!" he told them. And, like a visitation from hell, Cellur's metal vulture tore the eyes from its victims but left them living.

They had cut a path halfway to the knoll, yelling encouragement to its laboring defenders, when Cromis glimpsed among the many pennants of the Northerntribes the banner of the Wolf's head. He determined to bring it down, and with it whatever general or champion fought beneath it. He hoped—vainly—that it might be the Moidart herself. "Grif!" he shouted. "Take your lads on to the hill!"

He reined his horse around and flung it like a javelin at a wall of Northerners who, dropping their gaudy shields in panic, reeled away from the death that stared out of his wild eyes and lurked in his bloody weapon.

"Methven!" he cried.

He couched the butt of a dead man's pike firmly underneath his arm and used it as a lance. He called for the champion under the standard and issued lunatic challenges. He lost the lance, in a Northman's belly.

He killed a score of frightened men. He was mad with the horror of his own bloodlust. He saw no faces on the ones he sent to hell, and the face of fear on all the rest. He spoke poetry to them, unaware of what he said, or that he said it in a language of his own invention—but his sanity returned when he heard the voice of the man beneath the Wolf's Head.

"You were a fool to come here, tegeus-Cromis. After I have finished, I will give you to my wolves—"

"Why have you done this?" whispered Cromis.

The turncoat's face was long and saturnine, his mouth wide and mobile, thin-lipped under a drooping moustache. A wrinkled scar, left long ago by the knife of Thorisman Carlemaker, ran from the corner of one deep-set gray eye, ruching the skin of his cheek. His black, curling hair fell round the shoulders of a purple velvet cloak he had once worn at the Court of King Methven. He sat his heavy horse with confidence, and his mouth curled in contempt.

"Waterbeck is dead," he said. "If you have come to sue for peace on behalf of this rabble—" Here, the surrounding Northmen howled and beat their hands together "—I may be lenient. The Queen has given me wide powers of discretion."

Shaking with reaction to his berserk fit, Cromis steadied himself against the pommel of his saddle. He was bemused. A little of him could not believe what was happening.

"I came here for single combat with Canna Moidart's champion. Have I found him?"

"You have."

The traitor nodded, and the Moidart's footsoldiers drew back to form an arena. They grinned and whistled, shook their shields. Elsewhere, the battle continued, but it might have been on another planet.

"What did she offer you? Was it worth the pain you caused Carron Ban?"

The man beneath the Wolf's Head smiled.

"There is a vitality in the North, Lord Cromis, that was lost to Viriconium when Methven died. She offered me an expanding culture in return for a dead one."

Cromis shook his head, and lifted the nameless sword.

"Our old friendship means nothing to you?"

"It will make you a little harder to kill, Lord Cromis."

"I am glad you admit to that. Perhaps it is harder for the betrayer than for the betrayed. Norvin Trinor, you are a turncoat and a fool."

With the jeers of the encircling Northmen in his ears, he kicked his horse forward.

Trinor's heavy blade swung at his head. He parried the stroke, but it had already shifted into a lateral motion which he was forced to evade by throwing himself half out of his saddle. Trinor chuckled, locked his foot under Cromis' left stirrup in an effort to further unseat him. Cromis dropped his reins, took his sword in his left hand and stuck it between the heaving ribs of the turncoat's mount. Blood matting its coat, the animal swerved away, compelling Trinor to disengage.

"You *used* to be the best sword in the Empire, Lord Cromis," he panted. "What happened to you?"

"I am ill with treachery," said Cromis, and he was. "It will pass."

They fought for five minutes, then ten, heedless of the greater conflict. It seemed to Cromis that the entire battle was summed up here, in a meeting of champions who had once been friends; and at each brief engagement, he grew more despairing.

He saw Carron Ban's hurt, disdainful face through the shining web of her traitor-husband's blade, but it gave him no strength; he understood that she had felt pity for him that night in Viriconium, knowing that this confrontation must take place. He saw also that he was unable to match the hate she felt for Trinor: at each encounter, something slowed the nameless sword, and he was moved to pity rather than anger by the sneers of his opponent.

But finally, his swordsmanship told, and in a queer way: Trinor's horse, which had been steadily losing blood from the wound in its side, fell abruptly to its knees in the disgusting mud. The turncoat kept his seat, but dropped his sword.

He sat there, absolutely still, on the foundered animal. The Northmen groaned, and moved forward: the combat circle tightened like a noose.

"You had better get on with it," murmured Trinor. He shrugged. "The wolves will have you anyway, Lord Cromis—see how they close in!—and the Pastel City along with you. They are a hungry lot.

"You had better get it over with."

tegeus-Cromis raised the nameless sword for the fatal stroke. He spat down into the face before him: but it was still the face of a friend. He shuddered with conflicting desires.

He raised his eyes to the ring of Northmen who waited to take his blood in exchange for Trinor's. He moaned with rage and frustration, but he could not drown out the voices of the past within him. "*Keep* your bloody champion!" he cried. "Kill him yourself, for he'll betray you, too!" And he turned his horse on its haunches, smashed into their astonished ranks like a storm from the desert, and howled away into the honest carnage of the battlefield as if the gates of hell had opened behind him.

A long time later, at the foot of the knoll in the center of the valley, two Northern pikemen unhorsed him, and wondered briefly why he apologized as he rolled from his wrecked animal to kill them.

*   *   *

"I could not kill him, Grif."

It was the second hour after dawn. A cold, peculiar light filtered through the low cloudbase, graying the dead faces on the corpse-heaps, striking mysterious reflections from their eyes. The wind keened in off the Waste, stirring bloody hair and fallen pennants. Four wallowing Northern airboats hung beneath the clouds like omens seen in a dream. The entire valley was a sea of Northmen, washing black and implacable against one tiny eyot of resistance.

Up on the knoll, Birkin Grif led perhaps two hundred of Waterbeck's troops: all those who had not died or fled into the Waste. A score of his own men still lived: their eyes were red-rimmed and sullen in worn, grimy faces. They stank of sweat and blood. They stared silently at one another and readied their notched and broken weapons for the last attack.

"I could not do it."

Cromis had fought his way to the top of the hill on foot, aided by Tomb the Dwarf and a handful of the smugglers. The metal bird had led them to him, hovering above him as he fought with the men who had unhorsed him. (Now it perched on his arm, its head and talons covered with congealed blood, and said: "Fear the *geteit chemosit*—" It had said nothing else since he reached the knoll, and he did not care.) He was smeared with other men's brains, suffering from a dozen minor wounds, and there was a pit of horrors in his head. He did not know how he had survived.

"At least you are alive," said Grif. His fat cheeks were sagging with weariness; and when he moved, he favored his right leg, laid open from knee to ankle in the death-struggles of his beautiful mare. "Trinor could have killed any of the rest of us with ease. Except perhaps for Tomb."

Of them all, the Dwarf had suffered least: hung up there on his dented exoskeleton he seemed to have taken strength from the slaughter; his energy-axe flickered brightly, and his motor-assisted limbs moved as powerfully as ever. He chuckled morosely, gazing out across the valley.

"I would have done for *him,* all right. But to what point? Look there, Grif: that is our future—"

Out among the corpse-heaps, black, huge figures moved on a strange mission, a mechanical ritual a thousand years old. The *geteit chemosit* had lost interest in the fight. Their triplex eyes glittering and shifting as if unanchored to their skulls, they stalked from corpse to corpse. They performed their curious surgery on the lifeless heads—and robbed each Viriconese, like the dead smuggler in the Metal-salt Marsh —of his brain.

"They will come for us after the Northmen have finished," said Cromis. "What are they *doing,* Tomb?"

"They are beginning the destruction of an empire," answered the Dwarf. "They will hack the brains out of the Stony City and eat them. They will take a power knife and a spoon to Viriconium. Nothing will stop them.

"Indeed, I wonder who are the actual masters of this battleground—it is often unwise to meddle with the artefacts of the Afternoon Cultures."

"tegeus-Cromis should go at once to the tower of Cellur," said the metal bird, but no one listened to it.

Theomeris Glyn, the old campaigner, sat some distance away from the rest of the Methven, hoping to reinvigorate his sword by stropping it on a dead man's boot.

"I think it is starting," he called cheerfully. "They

have licked their privates for the last time down there, and gathered up their courage."

With a wild yell, the Northerners threw themselves at the knoll, and it shook beneath the onslaught. A spearcast blackened the air, and when it had cleared, pikemen advanced unimpeded up the lower slopes, gutting the survivors and treading in their wounds.

Behind the pikers came a never-ending wave of swordsmen, and axe-men, and berserk metal-prospectors from the northmost reaches of the Waste, wielding queer weapons dug from pits in the ground. The shattered, pathetic remnant of Waterbeck's expeditionary force fell back before them, and were overcome, and died. They hit the summit of the hill like some kind of earthquake, and they split the Methven, so that each one fought alone—

Tomb the Dwarf sniggered and swung his greedy axe. He towered above them, and they ran like rats around his silversteel legs—

Birkin Grif cursed. His sword was shattered at the hilt, so he broke a Northman's neck and stole another. He called to his smugglers, but all that brave and dirty crew were dead—

Old Glyn lunged. "You've never seen this one before," he cackled, as he put his hidden knife in, "eh?" His opponent was astonished—

Cromis ducked and rolled like a fairground acrobat. The metal vulture was above him, the nameless sword was everywhere—

They came together, and made their stand.

"Methven!" cried Cromis, and they answered him "Methven!"

Something in the gray air caught his eye, a movement beneath the cloudbase. But a blade nicked his collar-bone, and death demanded his attention. He gave it fully. When he next looked up, there were seven airboats in the sky where there had been four, and three of them bore the arms of Methvet Nian, Queen Jane of Viriconium. "Grif! Up there!"

"If they are couriers," said Grif, "they come a little late."

The crystal launches clashed with a sound like immense bells. As Cromis watched, the Northern squadron-commander closed to ram: but the sky exploded suddenly around his ship, and burned, dripping cold fire; and, tail-first and crippled, it dropped out of the sky. Faint violet bolts chased it down.

"There's a cannon aboard one of those ships," said Tomb the Dwarf wonderingly. "It is the Queen's own flight."

Confused by this sudden renaissance in the air, the Northmen drew back from their prey and craned their necks. The dying airboat ploughed through them and blew up, scattering limbs and bits of armor. Howling with rage, they renewed their attack, and the Methven on the hill were hard put to it.

Up above, one of the Viriconese boats left its sister-ships to a holding action against the remaining three northern craft, and began to cruise up and down the valley. But the Methven were unaware of this until its huge shadow passed over them, hesitated, and returned. Tomb crowed. He tore off Cromis' tattered black cloak with a huge steel hand and waved it about above his head. The airboat descended, yawing.

Ten feet above the top of the hill, it swung rapidly on its own axis, and fell like a stone. The energy-cannon under its prow pulsed and spat. A hatch opened in its side. Its motors sang.

It was a difficult retreat. The Northmen pressed in, determined to claim what was due to them. Tomb took a blow from a mace behind the knees of his exoskeleton: a servo failed, and he staggered drunkenly, flailing about him.

Cromis found himself some yards away from the open hatch, the old campaigner at his side. They fought silently for a minute.

Then Theomeris Glyn put his back squarely against a pile of corpses and showed the Northmen his teeth. "I don't think I'll come, Cromis," he said. "You'll need some cover." He sniffed. "I don't like flying machines anyway."

"Don't be silly," said Cromis. He touched the old man's arm, to show his gratitude. "We'll make it."

But Glyn drew himself up. His age sloughed away from him. He had lost his helmet, and blood from a gash in his head had clotted in his beard; his padded doublet was in ruins, but the pride in his face shone out clear.

"tegeus-Cromis," he said, "you forget yourself. Age has its privileges, and one of them is to die. You will do me the honor of allowing me to do that in my own way. Get into the ship and I will cover your back. Go. Goodbye."

He met Cromis' eyes.

"I'll gut a few of them, eh?" he said. "Just a few more. Take care."

And Theomeris Glyn, a lord of the Methven despite his years, turned to face his enemies. The last Cromis ever saw of him was a whirling rearguard of steel, a web such as he had been used to spin when the old king ruled, and his blood was young.

* * *

Trembling violently, blinded by the old man's courage, Cromis stumbled through the hatch. The metal bird rocketed in after him. It was still screaming its useless message of warning: he suspected that its mechanisms had been damaged somehow during the fight. He slammed the hatch shut. Outside, the Northmen were beating their weapons on the hull, searching for another entrance, grunting like frustrated animals.

The ship lurched, spun, hung five or ten feet off the ground. In the green, undersea gloaming of its command-bridge, lights moved like dust-motes in a ray of alien sun. Navigation instruments murmured and sang. "I'm having some trouble here," said the pilot, conversationally. "Still, not to worry." He was a rakish young man, his hair caught back with a pewter fillet in the fashion of the Courier Corps.

Birkin Grif lay on the vibrating crystal deck, his face white and drained. Bent over his injured leg, a woman in a hooded purple cloak was attempting to staunch the bleeding. He was saying weakly, "My lady, you were a fool to come here—"

She shook her head. Russet hair escaped her hood. Her cloak was fastened at the neck with a copper clasp formed to represent mating dragonflies. Looking at her, Cromis experienced a terrible premonition.

Sprawled in a tangle of silver spars at the base of the navigation table, Tomb the Dwarf struggled with his harness. His ugly face was frantic. "Take her up! Take her up!" he shouted. "Help me out of this, someone—"

"We can expect a bit of fuss when we get up there," said the pilot. "Ah. Got her. Do hold tight—" He opened his throttles. The ship began to climb steeply.

Cromis, stumbling toward the Dwarf, was thrown to the deck. He dropped his sword. He hit his head on the fire control of the energy-cannon. As he passed out, he recognized the woman in the purple cloak: it was Methvet Nian herself, the Young Queen.

We are all insane, he thought. The Moidart has infected us all with her madness.

7

Shortly after Cromis came to his senses, the airboat was rammed.

Clinging grimly to a staunchion as the daring young Courier flung his ship about the dangerous sky, he felt as if he were sitting behind the eyes of a tumbler pigeon: earth and air blurred together in a whirling mandala of brown and gray, across which flickered the deadly silhouettes of the Northern airboats. He was aware that Tomb had finally escaped the embrace of his own armor; that Grif and the Young Queen had wedged themselves against the rear bulkhead of the command-bridge.

But his concern with events was abstract—since he could in no way influence the situation—and he had something else to occupy his mind: a speculation, a fear stimulated by the sudden appearance of Methvet Nian—

Abruptly, the portholes darkened. The ship gave a great shudder, and, with a sound like destroyed bells, its entire prow was torn off. Shards of crystal spat and whirred in the gloom. Five feet in front of the pilot, leaving his controls undamaged only by some freak of chance, an enormous hole opened in the hull: through it could be seen briefly the tumbling, receding wreck of the craft that had accomplished the ramming. An icy wind rushed in, howling.

"Oh," murmured the courier. A twelve inch spike of crystal had split his skull. Three fingers could have been got in the wound with ease. He swayed. "We still have power—if anybody can fly this thing—" he said, puzzledly. "I am sorry, My Lady—I don't seem to be—" He fell out of his seat.

Tomb the Dwarf scuttled on all fours across the listing deck to take his place. He fired off the energy-cannon, but it tore itself away from the wreckage. "Benedict Paucemanly should see me now," he said. He turned the ship in a wide loop, swung once over the battlefield. He flogged and cajoled it and nursed it over the Waste, losing height. Beneath the cloudbase, the sole uncrippled ship of the Queen's Flight fought a doomed action against the two remaining Northerners.

"Look down there," said Tomb, as they veered over the scene of Waterbeck's rout. "What do you think of that?"

The valley was a gaping wound filled with Northerners and dead men and thick white smoke which surged up from wrecked airboats, obscuring the dark figures of the *geteit chemosit* as they performed their acts of skull-rape. The Waste surrounding the battlefield was crawling with reptiles: hundreds of stiff, dust-colored forms, converging slowly from south, east and west, their motions stilted and strange.

"Every lizard in the Great Brown Waste must be down there. What are they doing?"

"They seem to be watching," said Cromis. "Nothing else." And, indeed, the ridges that flanked the valley were already lined with them, their stony heads unmoving as they gazed at the ruin, their limbs held rigid like those of spectators at some morbid religious observance.

"We fascinate them," said Birkin Grif bitterly. With the boat's return to stability, he had regained his feet. His leg was still bleeding freely. "They are amazed by our propensity for self-destruction." He laughed hollowly. "Tomb, how far can we get in this machine?"

The ship drifted aimlessly, like a waterbird on a quiet current. The Waste moved below, haunted by the gathering reptiles.

"Duirinish," said the Dwarf. "Or Drunmore. We could not make Viriconium, even if Paucemanly had postponed his flight to the Moon, and sat here at the controls in my place."

Methvet Nian was kneeling over the dead courier, closing his eyes. Her hood was thrown back and her autumn-rowan hair cascaded about her face. Cromis turned from the strange sight of the monitor-lizards, his earlier fears returning as he looked at her.

"There is nothing for us in Duirinish," he said, addressing himself only partly to Tomb. "Shortly, it will fall. And I fear that there is little point in our going to the Pastel City." He shook his head. "I suspect you had a reason for coming here, Your Majesty—?"

Her violet eyes were wide, shocked. He had never

seen anything so beautiful or so sad. He was overcome, and covered his emotion by pretending to hunt in the wreckage of the cabin for his sword.

He came upon the limp carcass of Cellur's metal vulture: like the young Courier, it had been torn open by a shard of crystal; its eyes were lifeless, and pieces of tiny, precise machinery spilled out of its breast when he picked it up. He felt an absurd sympathy for it. He wondered if so perfect an imitation of organic life might feel a perfect imitation of pain. He smoothed the huge pinions of its wings.

"Yes, Lord Cromis," whispered the Young Queen. "This morning, the rebels rose again. Canna Moidart will find resistance only in Duirinish. Viriconium is in the hands of her supporters—

"My Lords," she appealed, "what will become of those people? They have embraced a viper—"

And she wept openly.

"They will be bitten," said Birkin Grif. "They were not worthy of you, Queen Jane."

She wiped her eyes. The Rings of Neap glittered on her thin fingers. She drew herself up straight and gazed steadily at him.

"You are too harsh, Birkin Grif. Perhaps the failure was not in them, but in their Queen."

They drifted for some hours over the Waste, heading south. Tomb the Dwarf nursed his failing vehicle with a skill almost matching that of his tutor and master (no one knew if Paucemanly had actually attempted the Moon-trip in his legendary boat *Heavy Star:* certainly, he had vanished from the face of the Earth after breaking single-handed Carlemaker's air-siege of Mingulay,

and most fliers had a fanatical faith in the tale . . .)
and brought them finally to Ruined Drunmore in the
Pass of Methedrin, the city thrown down by Borring
half a century before.

During that limping journey, they discussed treachery:

"If I had Norvin Trinor's neck between my hands, I
would break it lightheartedly," said Birkin Grif, "even
with pleasure, although I liked him once."

He winced, binding up his leg.

"He has blackened all of us," murmured Cromis.
"As a body, the Methven have lost their credibility."

But the Queen said, "It is Carron Ban who has my
sympathy. Women are more used to betrayal than men,
but take it deeper."

It is the urgent and greedy desire of all wastes to
expand and eat up more fertile lands: this extension of
their agonized peripheries lends them a semblance of
the movement and life they once possessed. As if seek-
ing protection from the slow southward march of the
Rust Desert, Ruined Drunmore huddled against an
outflung spur of the Monar Mountains.

In this, it failed, for drifts of bitter dust topped its
outer walls, spilling and trickling into the streets below every time a wind blew.

The same winds scoured its streets, and, like an
army of indifferent house-keepers, swept the sand
through the open doors and shattered roofs of the inner city, choking every abandoned armory and forge
and barracks. The erosion of half a millennium had
etched its cobbled roads, smoothed and blunted the
outlines of its ruins, until its once-proud architecture
had become vernacular, fit for its equivocal position
between the mountains and the Waste.

Even as a ruin, Drunmore was pitiful: Time and geography had choked it to death.

Towards the end of the flight, a wide rift had appeared suddenly in the deck of the airboat, exposing the ancient engines. Now, as they hovered over the city, flecks of colored light, small writhing worms of energy, rose up out of the crack, clung to the metal surfaces of the command-bridge, fastened on the inert carcass of the mechanical vulture, and clustered about the Queen's rings.

Tomb grew nervous. "Corpse lights," he muttered. He brought the machine down in Lnuthos Plaza, the four-acre field of Time-polished granite from which Borring had organized the destruction of Drunmore so many generations before.

Grif and Cromis dragged the dead courier from his ruined ship and buried him in a deep drift of loess on the southern side of the Plaza. It was a queer and somber business. The Queen looked on, her cowl pulled forward, her cloak fluttering. They were impelled to work slowly, for they had only their hands for shovels. As they completed the interment, great white sparks began to hiss and crackle between the shattered crystal hull and the surrounding buildings.

"We would be wiser out of this," suggested Tomb, who had been carrying out salvage work, as was his nature, and promptly rushed back into the wreckage to steal more tools and retrieve his exoskeleton. After that, they made their way through the bone-smooth streets until Grif could walk no further, the damp wind mourning about them and Tomb's armor clanking funereally as he dragged it along.

Under the one unbroken roof that remained (like a static stone haunting, like a five-hundred-year memory) in the city, amid piles of dust younger than the

Waste but older than the empire, they lit a fire and prepared a meal from the miserable stores of the wrecked machine. Shadows danced crudely, black on the black walls. The sun had gone down in a gout of blood.

At the prompting of some impulse he did not quite understand, Cromis had rescued the corpse of Cellur's bird from the ship. While they ate, he explained its nature to the Young Queen, and Tomb probed its mechanisms with a thin steel knife.

". . . We know nothing more of this man. But by sending the bird, he warned us—the fact that I did not heed the warning in no way devalues it—of the *geteit chemosit*. It may be that he has some way of dealing with them."

Birkin Grif chewed a strip of dried meat. He laughed.

"That is pure conjecture," he said.

"It is the only hope we have, Grif. There is nothing else."

"He is very clever with his hands," cackled Tomb the Dwarf, poking at the innards of the bird. He thought for a moment. "Or, like Canna Moidart, good at digging."

"So, if you do not object, My Lady, we will travel to Girvan Bay and solicit his aid. Should there be some secure place to which we can deliver you first—"

"Places do not guarantee security, Lord Cromis, only people—" Here, she smiled at him "—a thing we have both learned recently, I think—" He reflected ruefully that it was unwise to forget the astuteness of the House of Methven "—and, besides, I have been safe for seventeen years. I think I would like to be at risk for a while."

A huge, urgent lurching motion manifested itself on

the other side of the fire like a local geological disturbance. Birkin Grif had heaved himself to his feet. He looked down at the Young Queen, mumbling subterraneanly to himself. He bowed from the waist.

"Madam," he said, "you have the courage of your father. That is a brave attitude." He sat down again. "Mind you," he added in a low voice to Tomb, "it's a bloody long trip for a man in my condition."

Queen Jane of Viriconium laughed for the first time since she had lost her empire. Which shows at least, thought Cromis, the resilience of youth. He did not mean to condescend.

They stayed in that city for five days. A processing-center in the heyday of the Northmen, perhaps it welcomed the ring of Tomb's hammer as he worked on his damaged armor—a loop in Time, a faint, distorted echo from a past in which other mechanics had beaten the subtle artefacts of the Afternoon Cultures into cruder, more vital forms.

Grif's leg was slow to heal; exertion reopened it; the blood seemed slow to clot, and he found walking difficult. Like a convalescing child, he was prone to brief, silly rages. He limped and fretted about, railing at his own limitations. Finally, he forced himself to walk to the wreck in Lnuthos Plaza, tear a slim cobalt girder from the destroyed engine-housing, and bend it into a crutch.

It was an unfortunate admission. His gait thereafter was laborious, unsteady—and Tomb, a cruel humorist, imitated it gleefully, stumbling and capering like a crippled acrobat. That parody was a horrid work of art. Grif lost his temper, and implied that the power-armor was a less respectable kind of crutch. They went for one another murderously, all hooked hands and cunning blows, and had to be separated forcibly. They took to cutting each other dead in the bleak streets.

"You are preposterous," Cromis told them.

To Methvet Nian he said, "They are bored with inaction, we will leave here tomorrow"; but later that day two airboats bearing the Moidart's sigil ghosted in off the Waste and hung over the Plaza. Northmen swarmed down rope ladders to examine the burnt-out launch, kicked noisily through the wreckage, looking for souvenirs.

Cromis took his small party to earth in the archaic suburbs of Drunmore. But it became apparent that the airborne force was the vanguard of an attempt to re-occupy the city after half a millennium's absence; so they left the place that night, and went undetected into the cold spaces of the Pass of Methedrin.

They began their journey down the Rannoch:

It was a land of immense, barely-populated glacial moors, flanked by the tall hills—of bogs and peat-streams—of granite boulders split from the Mountains of Monar during slow, unimaginable catastrophes of ice, deposited to wear away in the beds of wide, fast, shallow rivers;

Of bright green moss, and coarse, olive-green grass, and delicate, washed-out winter flowers discovered suddenly in the lee of low, worn drumlins—of bent thorn and withered bullace, of damp prevailing winds that searched for voices in stands of birch and pine;

Of skylines, wrinkled with ridges;

Of heather and gorse, gray cloud and *weather*—of sudden open stretches of white water that would swell in Spring, dwindle and vanish with the coming of Summer—mysterious waterways;

It was green and brown, green and gray; it grew no crops; it constituted one quarter of the Empire of Viriconium.

At dawn each day, Cromis would leave his blankets, shivering, to inspect whatever snares he had set the night before: generally, he caught rabbits and waterlogged his boots: but he took a morose pleasure in these solitary outings. Something in the resigned, defeated landscape (or was it simply waiting to be born? Who can tell at which end of Time these places have their existence?) called out to his senses, demanded his attention and understanding.

He never found out what it was. Puzzling, he would return with his catch, to wake the camp and initiate another day of walking.

They were a ragged crew, a queer crew to be walking down the Rannoch like that: Tomb crucified in his leather leggings against the metal tree of his exoskeleton, never tiring, going like a machine over bog and river, leaping ravines and cutting down whole spinneys with his axe; Birkin Grif in the ruins of his splendid cobalt mail, hopping and lurching, cursing his crutch like a mad scarecrow; Cromis, his beautiful black hair lank in the damp wind, the dead metal bird dangling limply by its neck from his belt, stopping to gaze at waterworn stone by the hour—

And Methvet Nian in her purple cloak, discovering a portion of her lost Empire, and of herself. "Towers are not everything, Lord Cromis!" she laughed, and she took his arm. "They are *not!*" She brought him flowers and was disappointed when he could not identify them for her. He showed her crows and mountains, and expected no identification at all. He smiled; he was not used to that. They were thrown together by small observations.

In this way, they covered twenty miles a day.

During the third week, it snowed. Ice crusted the rivers, rock cracked and broke above the thousand-foot line of the flanking hills. Cromis found his traps full of white hares and albino foxes with red, intelligent eyes. Birkin Grif killed a snow-leopard with his crutch: for ferocity, it was an even match until the last blow.

For a week, they lived with a community of herders, small, dark-haired folk with strange soft accents, to whom the war in the north and west was but a rumor. They gave the Queen a sheepskin coat, they were shy and kind. As a measure of gratitude, Tomb the Dwarf cut wood from dawn to dusk; while Grif sat with his bad leg stretched in front of him, and split it into enough kindling for a year (they became friends again as a result of this: neither of them loved anything better than cutting and chopping).

Everything began to seem distant: the snow was an insulator: Cromis forced himself to keep in mind the defeat in the North. It was important to his brooding nature that he remember the terrible blades of the *geteit chemosit*. He imagined them. He saw them lay seige to Duirinish in his head. Would the winter halt them at all?

After seven days of that, and a further fortnight of travel in the grim mountains at the southern end of the Rannoch, he was glad to see the arable lands around Lendalfoot and catch a glimpse at last of the gray sea breaking on the dark volcanic beaches of Girvan Bay.

Lendalfoot was a fishing town built of pale fawn stone, a cluster of one-roomed cottages and long drying-sheds, their edges weathered, blurred by accumulations of moss and lichen. Here and there rose the tall white houses of local dignitaries. In the summer, fine pink sand blown off the shifting dunes of Girvan Bay filled its steep, winding streets; the fishwives argued bare-armed in the sun; and creaking carts carried the catch up the Great South Road into Soubridge.

But now the waves bit spitefully the shingle beach. The sea heaved, the mad black gulls fought over the deserted deep-water jetties, and the moored boats jostled one another uneasily.

Determined that news of the Young Queen should not travel North by way of the fish-route, Cromis sent Tomb into Lendalfoot to pose as a solitary traveler and gather certain information (he stumped off sulkily, stripped of his power-armor so as not to alarm the fishermen, but refusing to give up his axe) then retired with Methvet Nian and Birkin Grif to a barren basalt hill behind the town.

The Dwarf returned jauntily, throwing up and catching a small, wizened apple, which had been given to him (he said) by an old woman. "She was as dried up as her fruit," he laughed. "She must have thought I was a child." More likely, he had stolen it.

"It was a good thing I went alone: they are frightened and surly down there. News has come down the road to Soubridge." He crunched the apple. "The Moidart has taken Low Leedale, thrown down Duirinish—with great loss of life—and now marches on Viriconium.

"Between the Pastel City and Soubridge, the *geteit chemosit* are abroad by night, killing with no reason."

He ate the apple core, spat the pips imprudently at Birkin Grif—who was sharpening his sword with a piece of sandstone he kept in his belt for that purpose —and lay down on his exoskeleton. "They have given me directions, more or less precise." He strapped himself up, rose to his feet, once more a giant. He pointed out over the basalt cliffs, his motors humming.

"Our goal lies East and a little inland. The fishermen cooled further toward me when they learnt of my destination: they have little like of this Cellur. He is seen rarely, an old man. They regard him superstitiously, and call him 'The Lord of the Birds'."

8

In each of them had grown a compulsion to avoid roads and centers of population: by this, they were driven to travel the wilderness that stretches from Lendalfoot to the Cladich Marshes; a hinterland ruined and botched when the Afternoon Cultures were nothing but a dream in the germ-plasm of an ape; a stony wreckage of deep ravines and long-dormant volcanic vents.

"It is a poor empire I have," said Methvet Nian, "win or lose. Everywhere, the death of the landscape. In miniature, the end of the world."

No one answered her, and she drew her hood over her face.

It had not snowed in the South, but a continual rain lashed the gray and leafless vegetation, glossed the black basalt and pumice, and made its way in the form of agitated streams through the ravines to the sea.

At night, electrical flares danced about the summits of the dead volcanoes, and the columnar basalt formations took on the aspect of a giant architecture.

. As they went, they were shadowed and haunted by birds—ominous cruciform silhouettes high against the angry sky.

They reached the tower of Cellur in the evening of the second day. Cresting a ridge of pitted dolerite, they came upon the estuary of one of the unnamed rivers that runs from the mountains behind Cladich. Luminous in the fading light, the water spread itself before them like a sheet of metal. High black escarpments dropped sheer to its dark beaches; the cold wind made ephemeral, meaningless patterns on its surface.

Set in the shallows near the western bank was a small domed island, joined to the mainland by a causeway of crumbling stone blocks. It was barren but for a stand of white, dead pines.

Out of the pines, like a stone finger diminished by distance, rose the tower. It was five-faced, tapering: black. A tiny light shone near its summit, a glow that flickered, came and went. Birds wheeled about it, wailing mournfully, dipping to skim the water—fish-eagles of a curious color, with wings like cloaks in a gale.

"There is nothing for us here," said Birkin Grif abruptly. "Only a lunatic would choose to live here. Those fishermen had the right of it."

But Cromis, who understood isolation, and was reminded of his own tower among the rowans of Balmacara, shook his head. "It is what we came for, Grif. Those birds: look, they are not made of flesh." He touched the corpse of the iridium vulture hanging from his belt. "We will go down."

The estuary was filled with a brown, indecisive

119

light, the island dark and ill-defined, enigmatic. The creaking of the dead pines came clearly across the intervening water on the wind. From a beach composed of fine basalt grit and littered with skull-sized lumps of volcanic glass, they mounted the causeway. Its stones were soapy and rotten; parts of it were submerged under a few inches of water.

They were forced to go in single file, Cromis bringing up the rear. As they drew nearer the island, Tomb the Dwarf unlimbered his axe; and Grif, drawing his broadsword a little way out of its scabbard, scowled about him as if he suspected a conspiracy against his person on the part of the landscape.

With damp feet, they stood before the tower.

It had been formed in some unimaginable past from a single obsidian monolith two hundred feet long by seventy or eighty in diameter; raised on its end by some lost, enormous trick of engineering; and fused smoothly at its base into the bedrock of the island. Its five facets were sheer and polished; in each was cut twenty tall, severe windows. No sound came from it; the light at its summit had vanished; a stony path led through the ghostly pines to its door.

Tomb the Dwarf chuckled gently to himself. "They built to last," he said proudly to Cromis, as if he had personally dug the thing up from a desert: "You can't deny that." He strutted between the trees, his armor silver and skeletal in the dusk. He reversed his axe and thundered on the door with its haft.

"Come out!" he shouted: "Come out!" He kicked it, and his metal leg rang with the blow; but no one came. Up above their heads, the fish-eagles made restless circles. Cromis felt Methvet Nian draw closer to him. "Come on out, Birdmaker!" called Tomb. "Or I'll chop your gate to matchwood," he added. "Oh, I'll *carve* it!"

Soft but distinct in the silence that followed this threat, there came a dry, reedy laugh.

Birkin Grif cursed foully. "At your backs!" he bellowed, lugging out his heavy blade. Horrified by his own lack of foresight, Cromis turned to meet the threat from behind. Sweat was on his brow, the nameless sword was in his hand. Up above, the fish-eagles gyred like ghosts, screaming. The pathway through the pines yawned—a tunnel, a trap, a darkness. He aimed a savage overhand stroke in the gloom, a cut that was never completed.

It was Cellur of Lendalfoot who stood there, the Birdmaker.

The Lord of the Birds was so old that he seemed to have outstripped the mere physical symptoms of his age and passed into a Timelessness, a state of exaltation.

His long, domed skull was fleshless, but his skin was smooth and taut and unwrinkled; so fine and tight as to be almost translucent. His bones shone through it, like thin and delicate jade. It had a faint, yellow tint; in no way unhealthy, but strange.

His eyes were green, clear and amused; his lips were thin.

He wore a loose, unbelted black robe—quilted in grouped arrangements of lozenges—upon which was embroidered in gold wire patterns resembling certain geometries cut into the towers of the Pastel City: those queer and uneasy signs that might equally have been the visual art or the language or the mathematics of Time itself.

They had this property: that, when he moved, they seemed to shift and flow of their own accord, divorced entirely from the motions of the cloth of which they were a part.

"Hold your weapon, my lord," he murmured, as the point of the nameless sword hovered indecisively at his old throat. He eyed the dead lammergeyer dangling from Cromis' belt.

"I see by my bird that you are tegeus-Cromis. You have already left your visit too long. It would be a pity if you were to compound the error by killing the one you came to see."

He laughed.

"Come. We will go in—" he indicated his tower. "You must introduce me to your energetic friend with the power-axe. He would like to kill me, I feel; but he must save that pleasure. No dwarf likes to be made a butt. Ah well."

Stubborn Grif, however, would have none of it. When Cromis put up his sword, he showed no sign of following. He confronted the old man.

"You are either fool or malefactor," he said, "to risk death, as you have just done, for such a silly trick. In coming here, we have killed more men than you have eaten hot meals; and many for less than that practical joke.

"I should like proof that you are the former, senile but well-meaning, before I enter your house.

"How, for instance, would any of us know that you *are* Cellur of Lendalfoot, and not some reproduction as cunningly-fashioned as the bird?"

The old man nodded. He smiled.

"You would know by this, perhaps—"

He raised his arms and tipped back his head until he was gazing up into the darkening spaces where the fish-eagles flew. The diagrams on his robe appeared to fluoresce and writhe. From his throat he forced a wild, loud cry, a shriek compounded of desolation and salt beaches, of wind and sea—the call of a sea-bird.

Immediately, the eagles halted their aimless gyring about the summit of the tower. One by one, they folded their great ragged wings, and, returning the cry, fell out of the sky, the wind humming past them.

For a moment, the air about the Birdmaster was full of sound and motion. He vanished in a storm of wings: and when he reappeared, it was with an eagle perched on each of his outspread arms and ten more on the earth before him.

"They have been constructed, you see," he said, "to respond to a vocal code. They are very quick."

Birkin Grif sheathed his weapon. "I apologize," he said.

From the shadows by the door, Tomb the Dwarf sniggered quietly. He shifted his flickering axe to one shoulder, and came forward, his armor clanking dismally. He held out one huge metal hand to the old man.

"Fool or no, that is a trick I should like to learn." He studied the perfect iridium plumage of the birds. "We will make a pact, old man. Teach me to build such things, and I will forget that I am a sensitive and evil-minded dwarf. I am sorry I threatened to mutilate your door."

Cellur inclined his head gravely.

"I regret that it would have been impossible anyway. You shall learn, my friend. It is necessary that one of you be taught . . . certain operations. Come."

He led them into the tower.

It was an ancient place, full of the same undersea

gloaming that haunted the airboats of the Afternoon Cultures. There were ten floors, each one a single pentagonal room.

Three of these were given over to personal space, couched and carpeted; the remainder housed equipment of an equivocal nature, like the sculptures unearthed from the Waste. Light curtains hung and drifted; there were captured electrical voices whose function was obscure—

"Green," they whispered. "Ten *green*. Counting."

Tomb the Dwarf walked among them, his expression benign and silly. Suddenly, he said, "I have wasted forty years. I should have been *here*, not picking over the detritus of deserts—"

Incomplete carcasses of metal birds lay on the workbenches: there were eagle owls, and martial eagles, and a black-shouldered kite complete but inert, awaiting some powering-up ritual that would put life into its small and savage eye.

And in the last room, at the summit of the tower, there were five false windows, most precise duplicates of those that lined the throne room at Viriconium and showed landscapes to be found nowhere in the Empire . . .

There, after they had refreshed themselves, Cellur the Birdmaker told them in his dry manner of the *geteit chemosit,* and his own strange life:

I have (he said) waited for some time for your arrival. You must understand that there is very little time left. I must have your co-operation if my intervention in this affair is to become concrete and positive. I should have had it earlier. Never mind.

Now: you are aware of the threat posed to Viriconium by Canna Moidart. You are not, however, aware of the more basic threat implicit in her use of what the Northmen—from their trough of ignorance and superstition—have called *geteit chemosit,* that is to say, "the brain stealers."

This threat I must make clear: to do that—and, simultaneously, to set your minds at rest about my own position—I must tell you a little about myself and my queer abode. Please, sir, do not interrupt. It will speed things if you save your questions until I have outlined the broad picture.

Well.

Firstly, I want to make it clear that my involvement in this war is in no way political: the victory of Viriconium is as unimportant to me as the victory of the Northmen, except in one particular—please, Lord Grif, sit down and listen—with which I shall deal presently.

What concerns me is the preservation of the human race on Earth, by which I mean, on this continent, for they are one and the same thing.

Certainly, you may ask who I am, my lord—

It is my tragedy that I do not know. I have forgotten. I do not know when I came to this tower, only that I have been here for at least a millennium.

I have no doubt that I was here during the collapse of what you would call the Afternoon Cultures—that, at that time, I had already been here for at least a century. But I cannot remember if I actually belong to that rather mysterious race. They are lost to me, as they are to you.

I have no doubt also that I am either immortal or cursed with an extreme longevity: but the secret of that is lost in Time. Whether it was a disease that struck me, or a punishment that was conferred upon me, I do not know. My memory extends reliably for perhaps two hundred years into the past. No further.

That is the curse of the thing, you see: the memory does not last. There is little enough space in one skull for a lifetime's memories. And no room at all for those of a millennium.

I do not even remember if I am a man.

Many races came—or were brought despite themselves—to Earth in the prime of the Departed Cultures. Some stayed, marooned by the swift collapse of the environment that gave rise to the Rust Deserts, caught when the global economy could no longer support a technology and the big ships ceased to fly.

At least two of them survived that collapse, and have since successfully adapted to our conditions.

It may be that I represent a third.

However.

That is secondary to our purpose here. If you will consider the screens that face you, I will attempt to give you some idea of what we may expect from the mechanical servants of the Old Queen.

Yes, madam, the "windows," as you call them, have been here at least as long as myself. I may have constructed them, I cannot remember. Until I discovered certain properties of light and sound, they, too, showed only fixed views of places not to be found in the kingdom. Now, each one is connected—by a principle of which I have recently gained a little understanding—to the eyes of one of my birds.

Thus, wherever they fly, I see.

Now. We will operate the first screen. As you can see, Canna Moidart had little trouble in taking Duirinish—

The huge metal doors are buckled: they swing to and fro in a wind that cannot be heard. Beneath the over-

hanging walls, a mountain of dead, Northmen and Viriconese inextricably mixed. The battlements are deserted. Moving into the city, a patrol of scavengers, dressed in looted furs. Fire has blackened the squat armories of the city. On the edge of Replica Square, the Blue Metal Discovery lies in ruins. A dog sniffs at the still, huddled, headless figure in the center of the square. It is a dead merchant . . .

There, she left the small holding force we have just seen returning to Alves after a foraging expedition, and moved on to Viriconium—

The Pastel City. Five thousand Northmen march the length of Proton Circuit, their faces flushed with triumph. A tavern in the Artist's Quarter: spilt wine, sawdust, vomit. A line of refugees. The Pastel Towers, scarred in the final battle, when the last ship of the Queen's Flight detonated the power-source of the last remaining energy-cannon in the Empire, in a vain attempt to repeat Benedict Paucemanly's relief of the siege of Mingulay . . .

She was quick to move South. Here, we see the *geteit chemosit* in action against a group of guerillas, survivors of the Soubridge massacre—

That terrifying black skirmish-line, moving up a steep hillside, energy-blades swinging, in unison. The dead, sprawled about in agonized attitudes. A sudden close-up of a black, featureless face, three yellow eyes set in an isosceles triangle, unreadable, alien, deadly . . .

*   *   *

Mark that. That is the real enemy of Viriconium. I am sorry, Lord Cromis: I did not intend to cause Her Majesty so much distress. We will dispense with the fourth screen, my lady, and move on to the most important. This is taking place *now*, in Lendalfoot, the town you have just left—

Night. The unsteady flare and flicker of torches in the main street of the town. Their light outlines a group of fishermen, bending over something laid out on the cobbles. The scene jerks. An overhead view; a white, shocked face; tears; a woman in a shawl. There on the cobbles, a child, dead, the top of its head cut neatly away, its skull empty . . .

Finally, let us examine the history of what you know as the *chemosit*, and discuss my purpose in inviting you here. No, Lord Grif, I will be finished shortly. Please hear me out.

During a period of severe internal strife toward the end of the Middle Period, the last of the Afternoon Cultures developed a technique whereby a soldier, however hurt or physically damaged his corpse be, could be resurrected—*as long as his brain remained intact.*

Immersed in a tank of nutrient, his cortex could be used as a seed from which to "grow" a new body. How this was done, I have no idea. It seems monstrous to me.

The *geteit chemosit* were a result of escalation. They were built not only to kill, but also to prevent resurrection of the victim by destroying his brain tissue. As you remark, it is horrifying. But not a bad dream, those are not words I would use: it is a reality with which, a millennium later, we have to deal.

It is evident that Canna Moidart discovered a regiment of these automata in the north of the Great Brown Waste, dormant in some subterranean barracks. I became aware of this some years ago, when certain elements of my equipment detected their awakening. (At that time, I was unsure precisely what it was that the detectors *were* registering—a decade passed before I solved the problem; by that time, the War was inevitable.)

Now, Lord Cromis.

My tower's records are clear on one point, and that is this: once awakened, those automata have only one inbuilt directive—

To kill.

Should Canna Moidart be unable to shut them down at the end of her campaign, they will continue to kill, regardless of the political alignment of their victims.

The Old Queen may very well find herself in full possession of the Empire of Viriconium.

But as soon as that happens, as soon as the last pocket of resistance is finished, and the *geteit chemosit* run out of war to fight, they will turn on her. All weapons are two-edged: it is the nature of weapons to be deadly to both user and victim—but these were the final weapon, the absolute product of a technology dedicated to exploitation of its environment and violent solution of political problems. They hate life. That is the way they were built.

9

Silence reigned in the tower room. The five false windows continued to flicker through the green twilight, dumbly repeating their messages of distant atrocity and pain. The Birdmaker's ancient yellow face was expressionless; his hands trembled; he seemed to be drained by his own prophecy.

"That is a black picture—" Tomb the Dwarf drank wine and smacked his lips. He was the least affected of them. "But I would guess that you have a solution. Old man, you would not have brought us here otherwise."

Cellur smiled thinly.

"That is true," he said.

Tomb made a chopping gesture with one hand.

"Let's get to the meat of it then. I feel like killing something."

Cellur winced.

"My tower has a long memory; much information is

stored there. Deciphering it, I discover that the *geteit chemosit* are controlled by a single artificial brain, a complex the size of a small town.

"The records are ambiguous when discussing its whereabouts, but I have narrowed its location down to two points South of the Monadliath Mountains. It remains for someone to go there—"

"And?"

"And perform certain simple operations that I will teach him."

Cellur stepped into a drifting column of magenta light, passed his palms over a convoluted mechanism. One by one, the false windows died, taking their agony with them. He turned to tegeus-Cromis.

"I am asking one or all of you to do that. My origin and queer life aside, I am an old man. I would not survive out there now that she has passed beyond the Pastel City."

Numbed by what he had witnessed, Cromis nodded his head. He gazed at the empty windows, obsessed by the face of the dead Lendalfoot child.

"We will go," he said. "I had expected nothing like this. Tomb will learn faster than Grif or I, you had better teach him.

"How much grace have we?"

"A week, perhaps. The South resists, but she will have no trouble. You must be ready to leave before the week is out."

During the Birdmaker's monologue, Methvet Nian had wept openly. Now she rose to her feet and said:

"This horror. We have always regarded the Afternoon Cultures as a high point in the history of Mankind. Theirs was a state to be striven for, despite the mistakes that marred it.

"How could they have constructed such things?

Why, when they had the stars beneath their hands?"

The Birdmaker shrugged. The geometries of his robe shifted and stretched like restless alien animals.

"Are you bidding me remember, madam? I fear I cannot."

"They were stupid," said Birkin Grif, his fat, honest face puzzled and hurt. It was his way to feel things personally. "They were fools."

"They were insane toward the end," said Cellur. "That I know."

Lord tegeus-Cromis wandered the Birdmaker's tower alone, filled his time by staring out of upper windows at the rain and the estuary, making sad and shabby verses out of the continual wild crying of the fish-eagles and the creaking of the dead white pines. His hand never left the hilt of the nameless sword, but it brought him no comfort.

Tomb the Dwarf was exclusively occupied by machinery—he and Cellur rarely left the workshop on the fifth floor. They took their meals there, if at all. Birkin Grif became sullen and silent, and experienced a resurgence of pain from his damaged leg. Methvet Nian stayed in the room set aside for her, mourning her people and attempting to forgive the monstrousness to which she was heiress.

Inaction bored the soldier; moroseness overcame the poet; a wholly misplaced sense of responsibility possessed the Queen: in their separate ways they tried to meet and overcome the feeling of impotence instilled in them by what they had learned from the Lord of the Birds, and by the enigma he represented.

To a certain extent, each one succeeded: but Cellur ended all that when he called them to the topmost room of the tower on the afternoon of the fifth day since their coming.

They arrived separately, Cromis last.

"I wanted you to see this," Cellur was saying as he entered the room.

The old man was tired; the skin was stretched tight across the bones of his face like oiled paper over a lamp; his eyes were hooded. Abruptly, he seemed less human, and Cromis came to accept the fact that, at some time in the remote past, he might have crossed immense voids to reach the Earth.

How much sympathy could he feel for purely human problems, if that were so? He might involve himself, but he would never understand. Cromis thought of the monitor-lizard he had seen in the Waste, and its fascination with the fire.

"We are all here then," murmured the Birdmaker.

Birkin Grif scowled and grunted.

"Where is Tomb? I don't see him."

"The Dwarf must work. In five days, he has absorbed the governing principles of an entire technology. He is amazing. But I would prefer him to continue working. He knows of this already."

"Show us your moving pictures," said Grif.

Ancient hands moved in a column of light. Cellur bent his head, and the windows flickered behind him.

"A vulture flew over Viriconium this morning," he said. "Watch."

A street scene in the Artists' Quarter: Thing Alley, or Soft Lane perhaps. The tottering houses closed tight against a noiseless wind. A length of cloth looping down the gutter; a cat with an eye like a crooked pin flattens itself on the paving, slips out its tongue and devours a morsel of rancid butter. Otherwise, nothing moves.

Coming on with an unsteady rolling gait from the West End of the Quarter: three Northmen. Their leather leggings are stiff and encrusted with sweat and blood and good red wine. They lean heavily against one another, passing a flask. Their mouths open and shut regularly, like the mouths of fish in a bowl. They are oblivious.

They have missed a movement in a doorway, which will kill them.

As crooked and silent as the cat, a great black shadow slips into the road behind them. The immense energy-blade swings up and down. The silly, bemused faces collapse. Hands raised helplessly before eyes. Their screams are full of teeth. And the triangle of yellow eyes regards their corpses with clinical detachment . . .

"It has begun, you see," said the Birdmaker. "This is happening all over the city. The automata fight guerilla engagements with Canna Moidart's people. They do not fully understand what is happening as yet. But she is losing control."

Birkin Grif got to his feet, stared at the false windows with loathing, and limped out.

"I would give an arm never to have come here, Birdmaster," he said as he left the room. "Never to have seen that. Your windows make it impossible for me to hate the enemy I have known all my life; they present me with another that turns my legs to water."

Cellur shrugged.

"How soon can we move?" Cromis asked.

"In a day, perhaps two. The Dwarf is nearly ready. I am calling in all my birds. Whatever your Lord Grif thinks, I am not some voyeur of violence. I no longer need to watch the Moidart's fall. The birds will be more useful if I redeploy them over the route you must shortly take.

"Make sure you are watching when they return, Lord Cromis. It will be a sight not often seen."

Cromis and Methvet Nian left the room together. Outside, she stopped and looked up into his eyes. She had aged. The girl had fallen before the woman, and hated it. Her face was set, the lips tight. She was beautiful.

"My lord," she said, "I do not wish to live with such responsibilities for the rest of my life. Indirectly, all this is my fault. I have hardly been a strong Queen.

"I will abdicate when this is over."

He had not expected such a positive reaction.

"Madam," he said, "your father had similar thoughts on most days of his life. He knew that course was not open to him. You know it, too."

She put her head on his chest and wept.

For twenty-four hours, the sky about the tower was black with birds. They came hurling down the wind from the North:

Bearded vultures and kites from the lower slopes of the Monar Mountains;

Eagle owls like ghosts from the forests;

A squadron of grim long-crested hawk-eagles from the farmlands of the Low Leedale;

A flight of lizard buzzards from the reaches of the Great Brown Waste;

A hundred merlins, two hundred fish-hawks—a thousand wicked predatory beaks on a long blizzard of wings.

Cromis stood with the Young Queen by a window and watched them come out of night and morning: circling the tower in precise formation; belling their wings to land with a crack of trapped air; studding the rocks and dark beaches of the tiny island. They filled the pines, and he saw now why every tree was dead— Cellur had had need of his birds some long time before, and their talons had stripped every inch of bark, their steel bodies had shaken every branch.

"They are beautiful," whispered the Queen.

But it was the birds, despite their beauty, that destroyed their maker.

. . . For in the stripped lands South of Soubridge, where the villagers had burned their barns before the enemy arrived, a hungry Northman fired his crossbow into a flock of speeding owls. A certain curiosity impelled him: he had never seen such a thing before. More by luck than judgment, he brought one down.

And when he found he could not eat it, he screwed his face up in puzzlement, and took it to his captain . . .

Dawn came dim and grimy over the basalt cliffs of the estuary. It touched the window from which Cromis had watched all night, softening his bleak features; it stroked the feathers of the birds in the pines; it silvered the beaks of the last returning flight: seventy cumbersome cinereous vultures, beating slowly over the water on their nine-foot wings.

And it touched and limned the immense shape which drifted silently after them as they flew—the long black hull that bore the mark of the Wolf's Head and Three Towers.

Cromis was alone; the Queen had retired some hours earlier. He watched the ship for a moment as it trawled back and forth over the estuary. Its shell was scarred and pitted. After two or three minutes it vanished over the cliffs to the West, and he thought it had gone away. But it returned; hovered; spun hesitantly, hunting like a compass needle.

Thoughtfully, he made his way to the workshop on the fifth floor. He drew his sword and rapped with its pommel on the door.

"Cellur!" he called. "We are discovered!"

He looked at the nameless blade then put it away.

"Possibly, we can hold them off. The tower has its defences. It would depend on the type of weapon they have."

They had gathered in the upper room, Methvet Nian shivering with cold, Birkin Grif complaining at the earliness of the hour. Dry-mouthed and insensitive from lack of sleep, Cromis found the whole situation unreal.

"One such boat could carry fifty men," he said.

It hung now over the causeway that joined the tower to the mainland; like a haunting. It began to descend, slowed, alighted on the crumbling stone, its bow aimed at the island.

"Footmen need not concern us," said Cellur. "The door will hold them: and there are the birds."

Beneath the weight of the boat, the causeway shifted, groaned, settled. Chunks of stone broke away and slid into the estuary. In places, a foot of water licked the dark hull. Behind it, the hills took on a menacing gunmetal tint in the growing light. Cellur's fish-eagles began their tireless circling.

Five false windows showed the same view: the water, the silent launch.

A hatch opened in its side like a wound.

From it poured the *geteit chemosit,* their blades at high port.

Birkin Grif hissed through his clenched teeth. He

rubbed his injured leg. "Let us see your home defend itself, Birdmaker. Let us *see* it!"

"Only two humans are with them," said the Queen. "Officers: or slaves?"

They came three abreast along the causeway; half a hundred or more energy-blades, a hundred and fifty yellow, fathomless eyes.

The birds met them.

Cellur's hands moved across his instruments, and the dawn faltered as he lifted his immense flock from the island and hurled it at the beach. Like a cloud of smoke, it stooped on the *chemosit,* wailing and screaming with one voice. The invader vanished.

Blades flickered through the cloud, slicing metal like butter. Talons like handfuls of nails sought triplet eyes. Hundreds of birds fell. But when the flock drew back, twenty of the automata lay in shreds half in and half out of the water, and the rest had retreated to their ship.

"Ha," said Grif in the pause that followed. "Old man, you are not toothless, and they are not invulnerable."

"No," said the Birdmaster, "but I am frightened. Look down there. It seems to me that Canna Moidart dug more than golems from the Desert—"

He turned to Cromis.

"You must go! Leave now. Beneath the tower are cellars. I have horses there. Tunnels lead through the basalt to a place half a mile south of here. The Dwarf is as ready as he ever will be. Obey his instructions when you reach the site of the artificial brain.

"Go. Fetch him now, and go! His armour I have serviced. It is with the horses. Leave quickly!"

As he spoke, his eyes dilated with fear.

Despite repeated attacks by the birds, the *chemosit*

had gained a little space on the causeway beside their ship. In this area, four of them were assembling heavy equipment. They worked ponderously, without haste.

"That is a portable energy-cannon," whispered Birkin Grif. "I had not thought that such things existed in the Empire."

"Many things exit *under* it, Lord Grif," Cellur told him. "Now go!"

The tower shuddered.

Violet bolides issued from the mouth of the cannon. Rocks and trees vaporized. Five hundred birds flashed into a golden, ragged sphere of fire, involuntary phoenixes with no rebirth. Cellur turned to his instruments.

The tower began to hum. Above their heads, at the very summit, something crackled and spat. Ozone tainted the air.

Lightning leapt across the island, outlined the hull of the airboat with a wan flame.

"I have cannon of my own," said the Birdmaker, and there was a smile on his ancient face. "Many of those birds were so complicated they had learned to talk. That is as good a definition of life as I have ever heard."

The water about the causeway had begun to boil.

Cromis took the Queen's arm.

"This is no place for us. The old weapons are awake here. Let them fight it out."

The rock beneath the tower trembled ominously.

"Should we not bring the old man with us? They will kill him in the end——"

"I do not think he would come," said Cromis, and he was right.

* * *

Tomb the Dwarf was dull-eyed and bemused.

"I have wasted fifty years of my life," he said. "We must go, I suppose."

One hundred steps led to the caverns beneath.

It was a queer journey. The horses were skittish from lack of exercise, the tunnels ill-lit. Moisture filmed the walls, and fungus made murals from the dreams of a madman. Huge, silent machines stood in alcoves melted from the living rock.

The vibrations of the battle above died away.

"We are beneath the estuary. It is the underside of the world, where the dead men lose their bones."

They were forced to ride through a column of cold fire. They discovered these things:

The white skeletons of a horse and its rider; a sword too big for any of them to lift; an immense web; the mummified body of a beautiful princess.

Sounds that were not echoes followed them down the twisted corridors.

"I could believe we are out of Time," said tegeus-Cromis.

Finally, they came up out of the earth and stood on the lip of the Western cliffs, gazing down. The tower of Cellur was invisible, wrapped in a pall of colored smoke, through which the lightnings flashed and coruscated. The causeway had sagged, in places its stones were melted. Steam hung over the estuary.

A cold mist drew round them as they turned their horses South and West, making for Lendalfoot, and then the Forest of Sloths. As they left Cellur to his vain battle, one fish-eagle was hanging high above the smoke: circling.

Tomb the Dwarf never spoke to anyone of his sojourn on the fifth floor, or of what he had learned there. It

THE PASTEL CITY

is certain that he absorbed more than the knowledge required by his task, and that the Birdmaker found him an apt and willing pupil. Nor could he be persuaded to say anything of Cellur, the man who had forgotten his age and his origin. But in his later life, he often murmured half to himself:

"We waste our lives in half truths and nonsense. We waste them."

141

10

Canna Moidart's long thrust into the South reached Mingulay and guttered. The town fell, but in the bleak streets behind the sea-front, the *chemosit* sensed there was nowhere further to go: they slaughtered the civilians, and then, quite without purpose or emotion, turned on their masters, who died in a smell of blood and fish . . .

While, in the back alleys of Soubridge and the Pastel City, death wore precise, mechanical limbs . . . A greater war had begun . . . Or perhaps it had never finished, and the automata were completing a task they had started over a thousand years before . . . The Northmen desperately needed *enemies* . . .

"A forbidding prospect."

tegeus-Cromis and Tomb the Dwarf stood at the summit of a rainswept ridge in the South of that narrow neck of land which separates the Monadliath Mountains from the sea.

The country around them was alkaline and barren, an elevated limestone region seamed and lined with deep gullies by the almost constant rain: in areas, rock strata that had resisted the erosion of millennia made tall, smooth, distorted columns which stood out above the surrounding land.

"An old road runs through it, according to the Bird-master. What we seek is at the end of it—perhaps. You are sure you will recognize it?"

Above the grotesque spires and limb-shapes of the terrain, gray clouds were flung out across a drab sky, and the wind was bitter. Tomb tapped enormous steel fingers impatiently against the left leg of his exoskeleton.

"How many times must you be told? Cellur taught me."

They had been five days traveling. On the first night, the successful skirting of Lendalfoot and its un-easy garrison of Northmen, the fording of the major estuary of the Girvan Bay at low tide: but the next afternoon, crofters living in the south-western shadow of Monadliath had warned them of *chemosit* advance parties operating in the area, and their movements had been cautious thereafter.

Now, the vanguard of the South Forest barred their path.

The land sloped away from them for five miles, growing steadily less tortured as the limestone faded out. Low scrub and gorse made their appearance, gave way to groves of birch: then the black line of the trees—dark, solid, stretching like a wooden wall from the thousand-foot line of the mountains to the chalk pits by the sea.

"Well," said Cromis, "we have no choice."

He left the Dwarf staring ahead and made his way down the greasy Northern slope of the ridge to where Birkin Grif and Methvet Nian huddled with the horses under a meagre overhang, rain plastering their cloaks to their bodies and their hair to their heads.

"The way is clear to the forest. Hard to tell if anything moves out there. We gain nothing by waiting here. Grif, you and I had better begin thinking of our way through the trees."

Within half a day they were lost among the green cathedrals.

There was no undergrowth, only trunks and twisted limbs; their horses stumbled over interlaced roots, the going was slow. There was no movement or sound among the lower branches, only the slow drip of moisture percolating from the groined gray spaces above. Pines gave way to denser plots of oak and ash, and there was no path: only the aimless roads their minds made through the trees.

Mid afternoon.

In a clearing of gigantic, wan hemlock and etiolated nettle, Tomb the Dwarf left them.

"It is a bitch that I have to do your work, too," he muttered. "Stay here." And he strode off, chopping a straight route with his big axe, uprooting saplings out of spite.

Shaggy mosses grew on the Southern faces of the trees that ringed the glade; wet fungoid growths like huge plates erupted on their cloven massive trunks, bursting putrescently when touched. The light was lichen-gray, oppressive.

"We have come too far to the west," said Birkin

Grif, glancing round uncomfortably. "The land begins to slope." After a pause, he added in his own defense: "The Birdmaker was less than explicit."

"The fault is also mine," Cromis admitted.

Methven Nian shivered. "I hate this place."

Nothing more was said: voices were heavy and dead, conversation fell like turf on a grave, or the thud of hooves on endless leaf-mold.

At dusk, the Dwarf returned, a little less sullen. He bowed to the Queen.

"Tomb, my lady," he explained: "An itinerant dwarf of menacing demeanor. Mechanic *and* pathfinder—" Here, he glanced witheringly at Cromis and Grif, who had both become interested in a thicket of nightshade "—at your service."

He sniggered.

He led them to a poorly-defined path overshadowed by great rough blackthorn, the light failing around them. As the sun died without a sound somewhere off behind the trees and the clouds, they came to a broad, wasted space running to North and South in the mounting gloom.

Fireweed and thistle grew thickly there, but it could not disguise the huge, canted stone slabs, twenty yards on a side and settling into the floor of the forest, that had once made up a highway of gargantuan proportion. Nor could the damp moss completely obscure the tall megaliths, deeply inscribed with a dead language, that lined the way to the city in the forest: Thing Fifty, a capitol of the South in days beyond the memory of Cellur's marvelous tower.

They camped on the road, in the lee of an overgrown slab; and their fire, calling across Time, perhaps, as well as space, brought out the sloths . . .

"Something is out there," said Birkin Grif.

He got to his feet, stood with the flames flickering on his back, looking into the terrible silences of the forest. He drew his broadsword.

Flames and stillness.

"There," he hissed. He ran foward into the shadows, whirling the long blade round his head.

"Stop!" cried Methvet Nian. "My lord—leave them be!"

They came shambling slowly into the light, three of them. Grif gave ground before them, his weapon reflecting the flames, his breath coming slow and heavy.

They blinked. They reared on to their great stubby hind legs, raising their forepaws, each one armed with steely cutting claws. Patterns of orange firelight shifted across their thick white pelts.

Fifteen feet high, they stared mutely down at Grif, their tranquil brown eyes fixed myopically on him. They swayed their blunt, shaggy heads from side to side. Grif retreated.

Slim and quick as a sword, her hair a challenge to the fire, Methvet Nian, Queen and Empress, placed herself between him and the megatheria.

"Hello, my old ones," she whispered. "Your kindred sends you greetings from the palace."

They did not understand. But they nodded their heads wisely, and gazed into her eyes. One by one, they dropped to their haunches, and ambled to the fire which they examined thoroughly.

"They are the Queen's Beasts, my lord," said Methvet Nian to Birkin Grif. "And once they may have been more than that. No harm will come to us from them."

* * *

In two days, they came to Thing Fifty. It was a humbled city, ten square miles of broken towers, sinking into the soft earth.

Squares and plazas, submerged beneath fathoms of filthy water, had become stagnant, stinking lakes, their surfaces thickly coated with dead brown leaves. Black ivy clutched the enduring metals of the Afternoon Cultures, laid its own meandering inscriptions over bas-reliefs that echoed the geometries of the Pastel City and the diagrams that shifted across the robe of Cellur.

And everywhere, the trees, the fireweed, the pale hemlock: Thing Fifty had met a vegetable death with thick, fibrous, thousand-year roots.

Between the collapsed towers moved the megatheria, denizens of the dead metropolis. They lived in sunken rooms, moved ponderously through the choked streets by night and day, as if for millennia they had been trying to discover the purpose of their inheritance.

Tomb the Dwarf led the party through the tumbled concentric circles of the city.

"At the very center," he said, "a tower stands alone in an oval plaza." He cocked his head, as if listening to a lecture in his skull. "To descend into the caverns beneath the plaza, we must enter that. Certain defenses may still be operating. But I have the trick of those, I hope."

The ground sloped steeply down as they went, as if Thing Fifty had been built in the bowl of a tremendous amphitheater. They were forced to cross pools and unpleasant moats. Running water became common, springs bubbling from the cracked paving.

"I had not counted on this. The bunkers may be waterlogged. Run-off from the foothills of the Monadliath has done this. Help for the trees, but not us."

He was near the mark, but how near, he could not have imagined: and when they reached the plaza, none of his new skills were of any use.

For at the hub of the city of Thing Fifty lay a perfectly oval tarn of clear water.

At its center, like the stub of one of Tomb's own broken teeth, rose the last few feet of a tall tower. In its depths, they could see luxuriant water-plants rooted in the thick black silt that had covered and blocked the entrance to the bunkers.

Into their stunned silence, Birkin Grif murmured, "We are finished here before we begin. It is drowned."

Methvet Nian looked at Tomb. "What shall we do?"

"Do?" He laughed bitterly. "Throw ourselves in. Do what you like. I can accomplish nothing *here*."

He stalked off a little way and sat down. He threw lumps of dead wood and stone into the water that mocked him.

"We cannot get down there," said Cromis. "We will sleep in a drier part of the city tonight, and in the morning move on.

"Cellur told us that the siting of the artificial brain was uncertain. We had warning of that. We will try our second goal, in the Lesser Rust Desert.

"If that fails, we can come back here—"

Tomb the Dwarf sniggered.

"And dive like ducks? You are a fool. We have lost the game."

Cromis fondled the hilt of his sword. "We lost the game a long time since, in the Great Brown Waste," he said, "but we still live. It is all we can do."

"Oh yes indeed," said a soft, ironical voice from close behind him. *"It is your place to lose, I think."*

Cromis turned, horror blooming in his skull, his sword sliding from its leather scabbard.

Norvin Trinor stood before him.

Twenty Northmen were at his back, forceblades spitting and hissing in their hands.

"You should have killed me when you had the chance, my lord," he said. He shook his head theatrically and sighed. "Still, perhaps it was not meant to be that way." —

He looked from Cromis to Grif. The scar left by Thorisman Carlemaker's knife immobilized one side of his face, so that when he smiled only one eye and half his mouth responded. He still wore the cloak and mail Cromis had last seen on the battlefield. Like the leather garments of the Northmen, they were stained with blood and wine.

"Hello, Grif," he said.

Birkin Grif exposed his teeth.

"Arselicker," he said, "your lads will not save you, even though they kill me after I have gutted you." He showed Trinor a few inches of his broadsword. He spat on the floor. He took a step forward. "I will have your bowels out on the floor," he promised.

Cromis put a hand on his shoulder.

"No, Grif, no."

Trinor laughed. He swept back his cloak and slid his own blade back into its sheath.

"tegeus-Cromis sees it," he said. "Heroism is useless against a strategist: Methven taught us all that many years ago."

"You learned quickest of all," said Cromis dryly. "Grif, we could kill him four times over: but when we have finished, we will face twenty *baans*. Even Tomb could not stand against them.

"However well we fight, the Queen will die."

Norvin Trinor made a sweeping bow in the Young Queen's direction.

"Quite. A splendid exposition, my lord. However, there is a way out of this for you. You see, I need your dwarf.

"Let me explain. I am on the same quest as yourselves. I am able in fact to tell you that you are wasting your time here in Thing Fifty unless your interest is purely archaeological.

"For some time now, we have been a little worried about our allies. During certain researches in our Good Queen's library—" He bowed again "—in the Pastel City, I discovered what an unreliable weapon the *chemosit* are. Quite like myself, you understand: they serve only themselves. (Hold still a moment, Lord Grif. It will not hurt you to listen.) You have learned this, of course. I should like very much to know where, by the way.

"I came also upon part of the answer to the problem: the exact whereabouts of the machine which will . . . turn them off, so to speak.

"Now, I gather from your conversation here that the Dwarf has been given information I was unable to obtain. In short, I need him to do the business for me. I could not *take* him from you without killing him. Persuade him that it is in the best interests of all of us that he work for me in this matter, and I spare you. The Queen, too."

Throughout this monologue, Tomb had remained sitting on the edge of the tarn. Now, he unlimbered his axe and got to his feet. Norvin Trinor's wolves stirred uneasily. Their blades flickered. The Dwarf stretched to the full eleven feet his armor lent him and stood towering over the traitor.

He raised the axe.

He said: "I was born in a back alley, Trinor. If I had suspected at the battle for Mingulay that you would do this to three men who fought alongside you, I would have put a *baan* between your ribs while you slept. I will do your job for you because it is the job I came to do. Afterwards, I will cut off your knackers and stitch them into your mouth.

"Meanwhile, Methvet Nian remains unharmed."

And he let the axe fall to his side.

"Very well. We declare a truce, then: precarious, but it should not stain your finer feelings too much. I will allow you to keep your weapons." He smiled at Cromis' start of surprise. "But a man of mine stays by the Queen at all times.

"I have an airboat parked on the Southern edge of the city. We will leave immediately."

Later, as they entered the black ship, its hatch opening directly beneath the crude, cruel sigil of the Wolf's Head, Cromis asked:

"How did you discover us? You could not have followed us through the forest; or even through the barrens without being seen—"

Trinor looked puzzled. Then he gave his crippled smile.

"Had you not realized? It was pure luck: we were here before you entered the city. That's the beauty of it. We had stopped for fresh meat. At that time, I anticipated a long sojourn in the desert."

And he pointed to the great heap of carcasses that lay beside the launch, their white pelts stained with gore, their myopic eyes glazed in death. Crewmen were preparing to haul them into the cargo hold, with chains.

Cromis looked out at the tangled landscape of Thing Fifty.

"You are an animal," he said.

Norvin Trinor laughed. He clapped Cromis on the shoulder. "When you forget you are an animal, my lord, you begin to *lose*."

11

Brown, featureless desert slipped beneath the keel of the drifting airboat: the Lesser Waste, in all respects similar to the great dead region North of Duirinish, the spoliated remnants of an industrial hinterland once administered from Thing Fifty.

tegeus-Cromis, Birkin Grif and Tomb the Dwarf, locked in the cargo hold with the dead megatheria, paced restlessly the throbbing crystal deck. With a power blade at the neck of Methvet Nian, Norvin Trinor had forced the Dwarf to give up his armor, although he had allowed him to keep his axe. He looked like an ancient, twisted child.

"A chance may come when I breach the defenses of the organic brain," he said. He fondled the axe. He shrugged. "Indeed, I may slip, and kill us all."

The boat lurched in an updraft: white carcasses slid about the hold. Cromis stared from the single porthole down at the desert. Unknown to him, his fingers plucked at the hilt of the nameless sword.

"Whatever is done, it must not involve a fight. You understand that, Grif? I want no fighting unless we can be sure the Queen will remain unharmed."

Grif nodded sulkily.

"In other words, do nothing," he said.

As he spoke, the bulkhead door opened. Norvin Trinor stepped through, two of his wolves flanking him. He pulled at his drooping moustache.

"A commendable plan," he said. "Most wise." He looked at Grif for some moments, then turned to Tomb. "Dwarf, we have arrived. Look down there and tell me if this place was mentioned in your information."

Tomb moved to the porthole.

"It is a desert. Deserts were indeed mentioned to me." He showed his rotting teeth. "Trinor, you are displaying a traditional foolishness. I can tell nothing for sure until we land."

The traitor nodded curtly, and left. A few moments later, the airboat began to descend, bucking a little as it entered a low level of wind.

Trinor's pilot settled the ship on a bare shield of black rock like an island in the rolling limbo of the dunes. The engines ceased to pulse, and a soft, intermittent hissing sound commenced beyond the hull. Time is erosion: an icy wind blew streams of dust across the surface of the rock. It had been blowing for a millennium.

They stood in the lee of the vehicle, eddies of wind wrapping their cloaks about them. Dust in their eyes and mouths. Cromis looked at the thin, hunched shoulders of the Queen. We are nothing but eroded men, he thought, Wind clothing our eyes with white ice. Benedict Paucemanly flew to the *Earth*. It is we who live on the barren Moon . . .

"Well?" said Trinor.

A hundred yards away reared the curving flank of a dune. From it poked the ends of broken and melted load girders, like a grove of buckled steel trees. They were bright, polished and eroded. Cromis, eyeing the desolation silently, became aware that beneath the muted cry of the archaic wind was a low humming: the rock beneath his feet was vibrating faintly.

Tomb the Dwarf walked about. He bent down and put his ear to the rock. He got up again and dusted his leather leggings.

"This is the place," he said. "Begin digging at the base of the dune." He grinned cockily at Cromis. "The wolves become moles," he said loudly. "This would have taken us weeks without them. Perhaps we should thank Lord Traitor." He strutted off to examine the girder-forest, his long white hair knotting in the wind.

With surly grunts, the Northmen were set to work; and by noon of the following day, their labors had exposed a rectangular doorway in the flank of the dune: a long low slit sealed with a slab of the same resistant obsidian stuff as had been used to construct the Birdmaker's tower.

The maker of the door had cut deep ideographs in it. Time and the desert had been unable to equal him in this respect: the slab was as smooth and the ciphers as precise as if they had been made the day before. It seemed a pity that no one could read them.

Trinor was jubilant.

"We have a door," he said, pulling at his moustache.

"Now let us see if our dwarf can provide a key." He slapped Tomb jovially on the shoulder.

"You forget yourself," murmured the Dwarf.

He stood before the door, his lips moving silently. Perhaps he was recalling his apprenticeship on the fifth floor. He knelt. He passed his hands over a row of ideographs. A red glow sprang up and followed them. He murmured something: repeated it.

"NEEDS YOU," intoned the door abruptly, in a precise, hollow voice: "NEEDS YOU, BAA, BAA, BAA. OURUBUNDOS—"

The gathered Northmen dropped their spades. Many of them made religious signs with their fingers. Eyes round, they clutched their weapons, breathing through their open mouths.

"DOG MOON, DOG YEARS," moaned the door: "BAA, BAA, BAA."

And to each ritualistic syllable, Tomb made a suitable reply. Their dialogue lasted for some minutes before silence descended and he began again the process of moving his hands across the ancient script.

"GOLEBOG!" screamed the door.

A brief, intense flare of white light obscured the Dwarf. He staggered out of it, beating at his clothes. He chuckled. His hair reeked, his leggings smoldered. He blew on his fingers.

"The door mechanism has become insane over the years," he said. "It—" Here, he said a word that no one knew "—me, but I misled it. Look."

Slowly, and with no sound, the obsidian slab had hinged downwards, until it rested like the lower lip of a slack mechanical mouth on the dust, compacting it; and behind it stretched a sloping corridor lit by a pale, shifting pastel glow.

"Your door is open," he told Trinor. "The defenses are down."

Trinor rubbed the scar on his cheek.

"One hopes that they are," he said. "tegeus-Cromis enters first. If there should be a misunderstanding between him and the door, the Queen will follow."

There were no accidents.

As Cromis entered the bunker, the door whispered malevolently to him, but it left him alone. The light shifted frequency several times as he stood there staring at the vanishing-point of the gently-sloping passage. Vague, unidentifiable musical sounds were all around him. Growing from the walls were clumps of crystal that reminded him of the Metal-salt Marsh; they pulsed regularly.

He felt no fear.

"Remain where you are, Lord Cromis." Trinor's voice seemed muffled, distant, as though affected by passage through the open door. "I shall expect to find you when I come through—"

He entered with sword drawn. He grinned.

"Just in case you had planned . . . Well, of course, I'm sure you hadn't." He raised his voice. "Bring the Queen through first."

When they had assembled, the Northmen sullen and silent, keeping their eyes fixed on the floor and mis-hearing their orders, he made Tomb take the lead. "Any . . . defenses . . . you should disarm. Remember where the knife is held, Dwarf, and who holds it."

That corridor stretched for two miles into the earth. Shortly after they had begun to walk, they found that the incline had leveled off. The nature of the walls changed: the clumps of crystal were replaced by yard-square windows, arranged at four foot intervals.

Nothing could be clearly discerned through them, but they were filled with a milky light in which were suspended vague but menacing organic shapes.

There were no turnings. Their footfalls echoed.

There were no junctions or side-passages. They did not speak.

They came eventually to a great circular chamber, in the center of which columns of light and great rods of shadow wove patterns impossible to understand, like spectral dancers at the end of Time. Its roof and walls, all of green diamond, made a perfect half-globe. Twelve corridors, including their own, led off it from twelve vaulting arches. Otherwise, it was totally featureless.

Those columns and cylinders of light and darkness flickered, intertwined, exchanged their substance, reversed their directions of motion. Motes of brighter light appeared suddenly among them, hovered like insects, and vanished. A single musical chord filled the place, a high cathedral resonance.

Cromis saw nothing he recognized as a machine.

"You had better begin," said Trinor to the Dwarf, looking uneasily about. His voice was taken by the diamond walls and flung about. As if in response, the visual display of the brain increased its activity. "It is aware of us. I would like to leave here as soon as possible. Well?"

For a moment, the Dwarf ignored him. His ugly features had softened, there was a gleam in his knowing eye. He was enraptured. He sniggered suddenly, swiveled slowly on his heel to face the traitor.

"My lord," he said satirically, "you ask too much. It will take a century to understand this." He shrugged. "Ah yes, you hold the knife, I remember." He shook his head sadly. "I can shut it down in a week—perhaps a little more. It is a matter of finding the right . . . combination. A week: no less."

Trinor fingered his scar.

For the next few days, Cromis saw nothing of Tomb or the Queen: they were kept in the central chamber of the complex, constantly under the eyes and swords of the reluctant Northmen, while he and Grif were limited to the cargo hold of the airboat, and lived out a dreary captivity among the dead sloths.

Each day, a Northman brought them food.

Cromis' in-turning nature enabled him to come to terms with this—he made verses while gazing from the porthole at the unchanging waste: but it betrayed him also in the end, in that it kept him unaware of Birkin Grif's shift of mood.

Confinement chafed the big Methven. He grew irritable and posed questions without answer. "How long do you suppose we will live after the shutdown? Tell me that." And: "The Dwarf cares only for his machines. Are we to rot here?"

He took to sharpening his broadsword twice a day.

Later, he lay morose and withdrawn on a pile of bloody pelts, humming songs of defiance. He tapped his fingers dangerously.

Each day, a Northman brought them food.

On the sixth day after the discovery of the central chamber, Birkin Grif stood behind the door of the hold, honing his sword.

The door opened, their jailor entered.

He had an energy-blade in his right hand, but it did him no good.

Grif stood over the folded corpse, eyeing with satisfaction its pumping stomach wound. He wiped his broadsword on the hem of its cloak, sheathed it. He wrested the flickering power-blade from its tightening grip. A terrible light was in his eye.

"Now," he said.

Cromis found himself dulled and slowed by horror.

"Grif," he murmured, "you are mad."

Birkin Grif stared levelly at him.

"Have we become cowards?" he said.

And he turned and ran from the hold, quick and silent.

Cromis bent over the ruin that meant death for the Queen. In the distance, cries of pain and surprise: Grif had come against the Northmen in the forepart of the ship, berserk.

The nameless sword in his hand, Cromis followed the trail of slaughter. On the command-bridge, three dead men. They sprawled grotesquely, expressions of surprise on their faces, their blood splashed over the walls. The place stank. The open hatch yawned. Wind blew in from the desert, filling the dead eyes with fine dust.

Outside, the wind tugged at him. A fifth corpse lay at the entrance to the bunkers. The door moaned and hissed as he entered. "OURUBUNDOS," it said. It snickered. Cromis caught up with Grif halfway down the corridor that led to the brain-chamber—too late.

His ragged cobalt mail was smeared with blood, his hands were red with murder. Over the corpse of his final victim, he faced Norvin Trinor. And behind the traitor, their blades spitting, stood ten Northern wolves.

Trinor acknowledged Cromis' arrival with an ironical nod.

"I did not expect quite such stupidity," he said. "I will make no more contracts with you. I see they are worthless."

Birkin Grif ground his heel into the chest of the dead Northman. His eyes sought Trinor's, held them.

"You have killed your Queen," Trinor said. "Yourself, too."

Grif moved a pace forward.

"Listen to me, Norvin Trinor," he whispered. "Your mother was had by a pig. At the age of ten, she gave you a disease. You have since licked the arse of Canna Moidart.

"But I will tell you this. There is *still* Methven enough in you to meet me now, without your dirty henchmen—"

He turned to the Northerners. "Make a combat ring," he said.

Trinor fingered his scar. He laughed. "I will fight you," he said. "It will change nothing. Four men are with Methvet Nian. They have instructions to kill both her and the Dwarf if I do not shortly return to them. You understand: die or live, you or I, it will change nothing."

Birkin Grif dropped the stolen energy-blade and slid his broadsword from its scabbard.

The dead Northman was dragged away. In the strange milky light from the windows of the corridor, the combatants faced each other. They were not well matched. Grif, though a head taller, and of longer reach, had expended much of his strength in the cabin of the airboat: and his slow, terrible rage made him tremble. Trinor regarded him calmly.

In the days of King Methven, both of them had

learned much from tegeus-Cromis—but only one of them had ever matched his viperish speed.

They clashed.

Behind the windows, queer objects stirred and drifted, on currents of thick liquid.

Two blades made white webs in the air. The Northmen cheered, and made bets. They cut, and whirled, and leaped—Grif cumbersome, Trinor lithe and quick. Fifteen years or more before they had fought thus side by side, and killed fifty men in a morning. Against his will, Cromis drew closer, joined the combat-ring and marked the quick two-handed jab, the blade thrown up to block . . .

Grif stumbled.

A thin line of blood was drawn across his chest. He swore and hacked.

Trinor chuckled suddenly. He allowed the blow to nick his cheek. Then he ducked under Grif's outstretched arms and stepped inside the circle of his sword. He chopped, short-armed, for the ribs.

Grif grunted; threw himself back, spun round; crashed unharmed into the ring of Northmen.

And Trinor, allowing his momentum to carry him crouching forward, turned the rib-cut into an oblique, descending stroke that bit into the torn mail beneath his opponent's knees, hamstringing him.

Grif staggered.

He looked down at his ruined legs. He showed his teeth. When Trinor's sword couched itself in his lower belly, he whimpered. A quick, violent shudder went through him. Blood dribbled down his thighs. He reached slowly down and put his hands on the sword.

He sat down carefully. He coughed. He stared straight at Cromis and said clearly: "You should have killed him when you had the chance. Cromis, you should have done it—"

Blood filled his mouth and ran into his beard.

tegeus-Cromis, sometime soldier and sophisticate of the Pastel City, who imagined himself a better poet than swordsman, clenched his long, delicate fingers until their rings of intagliated, non-precious metal cracked his knuckles and his nails made bloody half-moons on his palms.

A huge, insane cry welled up out of him. Desolation and murder bloomed like bitter flowers in his head.

"Trinor!" he bawled. "Grif! *Grif!*"

And before the turncoat's hand had time to reach the energy-blade his victim had discarded—long, long before he had time to form a stroke with his arm, or a word with his lips—the nameless blade was buried to its hilt in his mouth, its point had levered apart the bones of his neck and burst with a soft noise through the back of his skull.

tegeus-Cromis shuddered. He threw back his head and howled like a beast. He put his foot against the dead man's breastbone and pulled out his blade.

"You were never good enough, Trinor," he said, savagely. "Never."

He turned to face his death and the death of the world, weeping.

"Come and kill me," he pleaded. "Just come and *try.*"

But the Northmen had no eyes for him.

12

His face fired up with hate and madness, the nameless sword quivering before him, he watched them back away, toward the chamber of the brain. So he kicked the stiff, bleeding face of their dead captain. He crouched like a wolf, and spat: he presented them with lewd challenges, and filthy insults.

But they ignored him, and stared beyond him, their attitudes fearful; and finally he followed the direction of their gaze.

Coming on from the direction of the door, moving swiftly through the milky light, was a company of men.

They were tall and straight, clothed in cloaks of black and green, of scarlet and the misleading color of dragonfly armor. Their dark hair fell to their shoulders about long, white faces, and their boots rang on the obsidian floor. Like walkers out of Time, they swept past him, and he saw that their weapons were grim and strange; and that their eyes held ruin for the uncertain wolves of the North.

At their head strutted Tomb the Dwarf.

His axe was slung jauntily over his thick shoulder, his hair caught back for battle. He was whistling through his horrible teeth, but he quieted when he saw the corpse of Birkin Grif.

With a great shout he sprang forward, unlimbering his weapon. He fell upon the retreating Northmen, and all his strange and beautiful crew followed him. Their curious blades hummed and sang.

Like a man displaced amid his own dreams, Cromis watched the Dwarf plant himself securely on his buckled, corded legs and swing his axe in huge circles round his head; he watched the strange company as they flickered like steel flames through the Northmen. And when he was sure that they had prevailed, he threw down the nameless sword.

His madness passed. Cradling the head of his dead friend, he wept.

When Methvet Nian discovered him there, he had regained a measure of his self-possession. He was shivering, but he would not take her cloak.

"I am glad to see you safe, my lady," he said, and she led him to the brain chamber. He left his sword. He saw no use for it.

In the center of the chamber, a curious and moving choreography was taking place.

The brain danced, its columns of light and shadow shifting, shifting; innumerable subtle gradations of shape and tint, and infinitely various rhythms.

And among those rods and pillars, thirteen slim figures moved, their garments on fire with flecks of light, their long white faces rapt.

The brain sang its single sustained chord, the feet of the dancers sped, the vaulting dome of diamond threw back images of their ballet.

Off to one side of the display sat Tomb the Dwarf, a lumpen, earthbound shape, his chin on his hand, a smile on his ugly face, his eyes following every shade of motion. His axe lay by his side.

"They are beautiful," said tegeus-Cromis. "It seems a pity that a homicidal dwarf should discover such beauty. Why do they dance in that fashion?"

Tomb chuckled.

"To say that I appreciated that would be a lie. I suspect they have a method of communication with the brain many times more efficient than crude passes of the hand. In a sense, they are the brain at this moment—"

"Who are they, Tomb?"

"They are men of the Afternoon Cultures, my friend. They are the Resurrected Men."

Cromis shook his head. The dancers swayed, their cloaks a whirl of emerald and black. "You cannot expect me to understand any of this."

Tomb leaped to his feet. Suddenly, he danced away from Cromis and the Queen in a queer little parody of the ballet of the brain, an imitation full of sadness and humor. He clapped his hands and cackled.

"Cromis," he said, "it was a master-stroke. Listen—"

He sat down again.

"I lied to Trinor. Nothing was simpler than dealing with the *geteit chemosit*. Those golems stopped operating twenty minutes after I had entered this room. Wherever they were, they froze, their mechanisms ceased to function. For all I know, they are rusting. Cellur taught me that.

"What he did not tell me was that a dialogue could be held with the brain: that, I learned for myself, in the next twenty minutes. Then—

"Cromis, Cellur was wrong. One vital flaw in his reasoning led to what you have seen today. He regarded the *chemosit* as simple destroyers: but the Northmen were nearer to the truth when they called them the brain-stealers. The *chemosit* are harvesters.

"It was their function in the days of the Afternoon Cultures not to *prevent* the resurrection of a warrior, but to bring the contents of his skull here, or to a similar center, and give it into care of the artificial brain. This applied equally to a dead friend or a foe actually slain by the *chemosit*—I think they saw war in a different way to ourselves, perhaps as a game.

"When Canna Moidart denied the *chemosit* their full function by using them solely as fighters, she invited destruction.

"Now. Each of the 'windows' in this place is in reality a tank of sustaining fluid, in which is suspended the brain of a dead man. Upon the injection of a variety of other fluids and nutrients, that brain may be stimulated to reform its departed owner.

"On the third day of our captivity here, the artificial brain reconstructed Fimbruthil and Lonath, those with the emerald cloaks.

"On the fourth day, Bellin, and Mader-Monad, and Sleth. See how those three dance! And yesterday, the rest. The brain then linked me to their minds. They agreed to help me. Today, we put our plan into effect.

"Twelve corridors lead from this chamber, like the spokes of a wheel miles in diameter: the Resurrected men were born in the north-western corridor. At a given signal, they issued from their wombs, crept here, and slew the guards Trinor had left when he went to his death. The fourteen of us stepped into the light-columus. From there, by a property of the brain-complex, we were—shifted—to the desert outside.

"We waited there for Trinor and his men. By then, of course, he was . . . otherwise involved. We eventually re-entered the bunker, and arrived in time to save you from yourself."

tegeus-Cromis smiled stiffly.

"That was well done, Tomb. And what now? Will you send them back to sleep?"

The Dwarf frowned.

"Cromis! We will have an army of them! Even now, they are awakening the brain fully. We will build a new Viriconium together, the Methven and the Reborn Men, side by side—"

The diamond walls of the chamber shone and glittered. The brain hummed. An arctic coldness descended on the mind of tegeus-Cromis. He looked at his hands.

"Tomb," he said: "You are aware that this will destroy the Empire just as surely as Canna Moidart destroyed it?"

The Dwarf came hurriedly to his feet.

"What?"

"They are too beautiful, Tomb; they are too accomplished. If you go on with this, there will be no new Empire—instead, they will absorb us: and after a millennium's pause, the Afternoon Cultures will resume their long sway over the Earth.

"No malice will be involved. Indeed, they may thank us many times over for bringing them back to the world. But, as you have said yourself, they have a view of life that is alien to us; and do not forget that it was them who made the waste around us."

As he gazed at the perfect bodies of the Resurrected men, a massive sadness, a brutal sense of incompleteness came upon him. He studied the honest face of the Dwarf before him, but could find no echo of his own emotion—only puzzlement, and, beneath that, a continuing elation.

"Tomb, I want no part of this."

As he walked toward the arch from which they had issued, his head downcast so that he should not see that queer dance—so that he should not be ensnared and fascinated by its inhumanity—Methvet Nian, Queen Jane of Viriconium, barred his way. Her violet eyes pierced him.

"Cromis, you should not feel like this. It is Grif's death that has brought you down. You blame yourself, you see things crookedly. Please—"

tegeus-Cromis said: "Madam, I caused his death. I am sick of myself; I am sick of being constantly in the wrong place at the wrong time: I am sick of the endless killing that is necessary to right my mistakes. He was my *friend*. Even Trinor was once my friend.

"But that is not at issue.

"My lady, we regarded the Northmen as barbarians, and they were." He laughed. "Today, *we* are the barbarians. *Look* at them!"

And when she turned to watch the choreography of the brain, the celebration of ten thousand years of death and rebirth, he fled.

He ran toward the light. When he passed the corpse of his dead friend, he began to weep again. He picked up his sword. He tried to smash a crystal window with its hilt. The corridor oppressed him. Beyond the windows, the dead brains drifted. He ran on.

"You should have done it," whispered Birkin Grif in the soft spaces of his skull; and, "OURUBUNDOS!" giggled the insane door, as he fell through it and in to the desert wind. His cloak cracking and whipping about him, so that he resembled a crow with broken wings, he stumbled toward the black airboat. His mind mocked him. His face was wet.

He threw himself into the command-bridge. Green light swam about him, and the dead Northmen stared blindly at him as he turned on the power. He did not choose a direction, it chose him. Under full acceleration, he fled out into the empty sky.

And so tegeus-Cromis, Lord of the Methven, was not present at the forming of the Host of the Reborn Men, at their arming in the depths of the Lesser Waste, or their marching. He did not see the banners.

Neither was he witness to the fall of Soubridge, when, a month after the sad death of Birkin Grif, Tomb the Giant Dwarf led the singing men of the Afternoon Cultures against a great army of Northmen, and took the victory.

He was not present when the Wolves burned Soubridge, and, in desperation, died.

He did not see the Storming of the Gates, when Alstath Fulthor—after leading a thousand Resurrected Men over the Monar Mountains in the depths of Winter —attacked the Pastel City from the north-east;

Or the brave death of Rotgob Mungo, a captain of the North, as he tried in vain to break the long Siege of the Artists' Quarter, and bled his life out in the Bistro Californium;

Nor was he there when Tomb met Alstath Fulthor on the Proton Circuit, coming from the opposite end of the City, and shook his hand.

He was not present at that final retaking of Methven's Hall, when five hundred men died in one hour, and Tomb got his famous wound. They looked for him there, but he did not come.

He did not break with them into the inner room of the palace, there among the drifting curtains of light; or discover beneath the dying wreck of Usheen the Sloth, the Queen's Beast, the cold and beautiful corpse of Canna Moidart, the last twist of the knife.

It is rumored that the Young Queen wept over the Old, her cousin. But he did not see that, either.

EPILOGUE

Methvet Nian, the Queen of Viriconium, stood at early evening on the sand-dunes that lay like a lost country between the land and the sea. Swift and tattered scraps of rag, black gulls sped and fought over her downcast head.

She was a tall and supple woman, clad in a gown of heavy russet velvet, and her skin was neither painted nor jeweled, as was the custom of the time. The nine identical rings of Neap glittered from her long fingers. Her hair, which recalled the color of autumn rowans, hung in soft waves to her waist, coiled about her breasts.

For a while, she walked the tideline, examining the objects cast up by the sea: paying particular attention to a smooth stone here, a translucent spiny shell there; picking up a bottle the color of dragonfly armor, throwing down a branch whitened and peculiarly carved by the water. She watched the gulls, but their cries depressed her.

She led her gray horse by its white bridle across the dunes, and found the stone path to the tower which had no name: though it was called by some after that stretch of seaboard on which it stood, that is, Balmacara.

Balmacara was broken: its walls were blackened, it was like a broken tooth; and despite the Spring that had brought green back to the land after a winter of darkness and harsh contrasts, the rowan woods that surround it were without life.

Among them in the growing gloom of twilight, she came upon the wreck of the crystal launch that had brought down the tower. It was black, and a wolf's head with wine red eyes stared at her from its buckled hull—quite without menace, for the paint was already beginning to peel.

She passed it, and came to the door; she tethered her horse.

She called out, but there was no answer.

She climbed fifty stone steps, and found that night had already taken the husk of the tower. Dusk was brown in the window arches, heaped up in great drifts in the corners. Her footsteps echoed emptily, but there was a strange, quiet music in the tower, a mournful, steely mode, cadences that brought tears to her violet eyes.

He sat on a wall-bed covered with blue embroidered silks. Around him on the walls hung trophies: a powered battle-axe he had got from his friend Tomb the Dwarf after the sea-fight at Mingulay in the Rivermouth Campaign; the gaudy standard of Thorisman Carlemaker, whom he had defeated single-handed in the Mountains of Monadliath; queer weapons, and astrological equipment discovered in deserts.

He did not look up as she entered.

His fingers depressed the hard strings of his instrument; its tone was low and melancholy. He recited the following verse, which he had composed on the Cruachan Ridge in Monar:

"Strong visions: I have strong visions of this place in the empty times . . . Far below there are wavering pines . . . I left the rowan elphin woods to fulminate on ancient headlands, dipping slowly into the glasen seas of evening . . . On the devastated peaks of hills we ease the barrenness into our thin bones like a foot into a tight shoe . . . The narrative of this place: other than the smashed arris of the ridge there are only sad winds and silences. . . . I lay on the cairn one more rock. . . . I am possessed by Time . . ."

When he had finished, she said, "My lord, we waited for you to come."

In the gloom, he smiled. He still wore his torn cloak, his ragged, dented shirt of mail. The nameless sword was at his side. He had this mannerism: that when he was worried or nervous, his hand strayed out unknown to him and caressed its hilt.

He said with the grave politeness of his time, "Lady, I would have come had I felt there was any need for me."

"Lord Cromis," she answered, "you are absurd." She laughed, and did not let him see her pity. "Death brought you here to sulk and bite yourself like an animal. In Viriconium, we have ceased to brood on death."

"That is your choice, madam."

"The Reborn Men are among us: they give us new arts, new perspectives; and from us they learn how to live in a land without despoiling it. If it brings you satisfaction, Cromis, you were correct—the Empire is dead.

"But so are the Afternoon Cultures. And something wholly new has replaced them both."

He rose, and went to the window. His tread was silent and swift. He faced her, and the sun bled to death behind him.

"Is there room in this New Empire for an involuntary assassin?" he asked. "Is there?"

"Cromis, you are a fool." And she would allow him no answer to that.

Later, he made her look at the Name Stars.

"There," he said. "You will not deny this: no one who came after could read what is written there. All empires gutter, and leave a language their heirs cannot understand."

She smiled up at him, and pushed her hair back from her face.

"Alstath Fulthor the Reborn Man could tell you what it means," she said.

"It is important to my nature," he admitted, "that it remain a mystery to me. If you will command him to keep a close mouth, I will come back."